AN ANGEL CALLED GALLAGHER

A Montana Gallagher Novel
Book Four

MK MCCLINTOCK

Cambron Press

Cambron Press
Bigfork, Montana 59911
www.mkmcclintock.com

McClintock, MK
An Angel Called Gallagher; novel/MK McClintock
ISBN-13: 978-0-9970890-8-0
ISBN-10: 0-9970890-8-3

Cover design by MK McClintock

"All Through the Night" lullaby lyrics written by Sir Harold Boulton in 1884. Original Welsh lyrics for Ar Hyd y Nos written by John Ceiriog Hughes.

Printed in the United States of America

PRAISE FOR
THE MONTANA GALLAGHERS

"The Montana Gallagher Collection is adventurous and romantic with scenes that transport you into the Wild West."
—*InD'Tale Magazine*

"Any reader who loves Westerns, romances, historical fiction or just a great read would love this book, and I am pleased to be able to very highly recommend it. This is the first book I've read by this author, but it certainly won't be the last. Do yourself a favor and give it a chance!" —*Reader's Favorite* on *Gallagher's Pride*

"*Journey to Hawk's Peak* by MK McClintock is one of the most gripping and thrilling western novels that anyone will ever read. This is probably the best novel that I have yet read as a reviewer. It clicks on all cylinders—grammar, punctuation, plot, characterization, everything. This novel is a serious page-turner, and for fans of western fiction, it is a must-read." —*Reader's Favorite*

"MK McClintock has the ability to weave the details into a story that leave the reader enjoying the friendship of the characters. The covers of the books draw you in, but the story and the people keep you there." —*My Life, One Story at a Time*

To learn more about MK McClintock and her books,
please visit www.mkmcclintock.com.

For Christmas angels and their families.
May you never forget the love and hope which binds your
hearts.

AUTHOR'S NOTE

Dearest Readers,

I fell in love with the Gallagher family from their first words. The characters are flawed, likeable, and yes, sometimes infuriating, but they're real and true to themselves. This is more than just a series, it's a western saga. The series follows the Gallagher's romance, hope, and revenge over the course of several books—each one offering something new.

It should also be understood that I write fiction, not history. I do my best to stay true to the time in which the books are set, but I do take some leeway as a fiction author. I accept full responsibility for any major historical discrepancies. I hope you enjoy the story and the Gallagher family as much I do.

–MK

1

Briarwood, Montana Territory—December 1883

White clouds of warm breath snaked through the cold air. She held her hands in front of her mouth in an effort to bring heat to her stiff fingers. Fresh snow had covered the land while she tried to sleep, and she didn't want to sleep too long for fear that the small fire would dwindle. Two thin pieces of wood leaned against the inside of the small black pail. She tucked her feet under her legs and pressed them into her chest. The wool blanket was thin and only warm enough for a cool day, not bitter winter nights. When the sun dipped behind the mountains and the moon rose, the cold seeped past the blanket and into her bones.

Sleep came and went like fleeting dreams until the stars faded, and the small window by the door promised to reveal a rising sun over the mountain peaks. It would be a good day to gather more wood and branches from the forest floor. She looked to the two pegs above the narrow stone fireplace where her father's rifle used to hang. The emptiness in her stomach might be worse if her father hadn't left behind a cut of deer. She finished the last of the meat the night before, and the gnawing in her gut told her she'd have to find a meal soon.

Her eyes closed when the soft rays of sun touched her skin. As though drawn toward the promise of warmth, she stepped off the bed with the blanket wrapped around her small shoulders and opened the front door.

Catherine Rose Carr had been raised properly and prided herself on her ability to do her numbers, read a full book without too much difficulty, and to follow the moral rules her mother said every young man and woman must abide by to get to Heaven. She wasn't certain if she was going to Heaven, or if her mother and father were even there waiting for her, but Catie was sure her behavior the past two weeks excluded her from ever finding out.

The snow soaked through her boots and left her legs weighed down with each deep step. Grateful she could find a moment of rest, Catie crouched low, pressing her back up against the wooden structure nearly the size of her cabin. She hadn't come this far to turn back now. It took almost ten minutes to convince herself that starvation was worse than stealing.

Catie hadn't been this far from the cabin before, and the ranch was the only place she'd come upon after half a day of walking through the woods. Her father had been adamant that she remain close to the cabin. Two days and he'd return—that had been his promise to her.

"Too many dangers beyond the walls of home," he had told her.

Catie didn't understand his concern. Hadn't he taught her how to shoot the Remington rifle? She might have had better success hunting if he'd left it behind.

Three weeks ago, she swore her father would not forget to return, yet as the days and weeks passed, she was forced to break her promise.

The chickens, who must have sensed the unknown presence,

squawked and squabbled from within. Catie covered her mouth with the end of the shabby wool scarf to keep any noise from escaping her lips. She heard the unmistakable sound of boots hitting wooden boards and someone talking softly to the fowl. Catie remained still as a sturdy oak, just the way her father had taught her when they tracked her first buck up the mountain. Someone else walked toward the chicken coop and entered the structure. Voices carried through the planks, and curious to know if they were friendly or a danger to her, she pressed closer against the wood.

"Brenna! You startled me. How did you manage to trudge out here in those boots, and what are you doing with a basket?"

"Then you startle too easily, Amanda."

The woman laughed, a light and lovely sound. She spoke differently than the other woman, almost like a song.

"My boots don't seem to fit well these days, so I borrowed an old pair of Ethan's. I wanted some fresh air, and since my aromatic oils should arrive any day now, I thought I'd gather some pinecones, give them a little scent, and set them around the house."

"What a nice idea. Would you like some company after I get these eggs back inside?"

"I was hoping you'd join me. I had a few ideas for the house that I wanted to discuss with you. I promised Ethan I wouldn't attempt to stand on anything when he wasn't around."

One of the women laughed, and Catie thought it was the other woman without the music in her voice. "Then we better not let him or your grandmother catch you."

Catie listened to the light rustling, and finally the door closed with the women on the outside. She shouldn't have dared. Reason seemed to have little place in her mind at the moment because she peeked around the edge for a glimpse. Starved for human companionship, Catie was desperate to call out. Almost.

When the women had disappeared around the other side of the barn, she trudged through the snow to the front of the coop. Careful not to disturb the chickens too much, she collected as many of the leftover eggs as she could carry wrapped in her scarf. Her gaze flitted over the hens once, and Catie shook her head.

"You're safe from me, little ones. I haven't fallen that far yet."

As quietly as she came, she disappeared back into the woods.

The unfamiliar voices halted Catie's progress into the rough-hewn cabin. Smoke rose from the narrow chimney, and the scent of cooked meat caused her stomach to clench. A smile formed on her red lips, though her happiness did not last. It appeared to be three voices and none sounded like her father. Catie held the eggs close to her chest and walked alongside the perimeter until she could comfortably peek inside the window.

Three men stood or sat in various stages of undress, snug in the nearly barren cabin. One of them turned something in a hot pan sitting precariously over the wood and coals in the fire, even as she wondered how they'd come upon her home so quickly. She looked into the sky where the sun shined directly above her. Her excursion to the chicken coop had taken longer than she realized.

She looked again at the men through the window, careful to remain out of sight. They'd used the last of the firewood. In the months she and her pa had lived in the solitary cabin, she'd not seen another soul come around.

Catie waited for each man to turn around so she could glimpse their faces. She was convinced none were her father now that she'd at least seen their backs, as much as she might have hoped otherwise. The third man turned, and an inaudible gasp escaped her lips. If ever there was a man in her past life she didn't want to meet again, it was him.

Catie pulled back, her eyes scanning the land around what used to be her home, or the home her father had found for them two weeks ago. Even if the men left, they knew where she lived. Looking down at the eggs bundled in her scarf, she ignored the pain of cold around her toes and walked back the way she had come.

She noticed the line shack in the distance. It was small, unoccupied, and warmer than the cabin. After a quick scan of the little room, Catie stepped inside, grateful to find a cot and a bin of wood for a potbellied stove. With the short winter days and the sun on a downward setting behind the mountains, she was out of options. Trespassing was only the latest in a growing list of wrongdoings. Survival demanded she forgive herself of the sin, and she prayed the owner of the shack would show mercy if they came upon her in the night. She didn't relish adding jail to her future list of shelters. With the simple hope embedded in her mind, she closed the door.

She set her precious eggs—the stolen eggs—down on the flat surface of the rough table and started a fire. The tinder was still dry, and after half a dozen attempts, a small flame licked the edges of the wood. A few minutes later, Catie's fingers turned a light shade of pink as the heat soaked into her skin, and she removed her boots to help warm her feet and dry her socks. The shack was better equipped than the cabin, and she found a small skillet and pot in a wooden box by the stove. A single plate, cup, and fork sat beneath the pan wrapped in a dusty cloth. She brushed the sleeve of her shirt over the pan to remove any lingering dust and cracked the eggs open when the heat seeped through the iron.

The eggs staved off the gnawing ache in her stomach, at least for one more night. Her hunger temporarily assuaged, Catie laid on the narrow cot, the scarf wrapped tightly around her shoulders. The few warm blankets were a blessing, and thankful for a sheltered place to rest, she fell into a deep slumber.

The following morning, Catie stood in the trees, her arms

filled with small branches for kindling. She watched a tall man dismount and circle the shack, look inside, and then return to his horse and rummage through his worn leather saddlebags. Her body shivered, and the trees offered little protection from the cold breeze. Light drops of wet snow fell from the low-hanging branches of the pine trees, testing the strength of her resolve. The man left the shack, remounted, and rode away.

She hurried back to the scant warmth of the shack and nearly tripped over her own feet. On the edge of the cot, a thick blanket was neatly folded. Her gaze darted around the small space, settling on the thick cut of beef on the table. Beside the beef was a clean, white towel. Catie pulled back the corners to reveal a dozen more eggs and half a loaf of bread. Why would the man leave them behind? How did he know she was there, and would he make her go away? She would worry over those questions in the morning. For tonight, she would feast.

2

Brenna Gallagher's eyes fluttered open. The heavy curtains blocked the cold and moonlight. Her husband's deep breathing always brought her a sense of security and comfort, except tonight something poked and prodded at her subconscious to awaken her.

She slipped from bed and into her robe. On stockinged feet, she walked quietly from the room and into the hall. Only the roar of the wind beating on the house filled what otherwise would be a silent night. Brenna took comfort in the great home's strength and foundation, but she knew firsthand that misfortune could penetrate its walls. They'd nearly lost her sister-in-law to her grandfather's hired man just a few bedrooms down from theirs. She quickly quelled the memory and stepped into the hall.

Brenna walked the short distance to young Jacob's room. With the events that had transpired over the past two years, it was a mother's over-protective instinct that drove her to look in on her son in the middle of the night.

Jacob was like his uncle Gabriel—Ethan's brother—and tended to sleep through almost anything. It wasn't his cries or quiet murmurs that drew her to the nursery door, but the sound of a familiar tune sung by a soft voice.

Angels watching, e'er around thee,
All through the night
Midnight slumber close surround thee,
All through the night
Soft the drowsy hours are creeping,
Hill and dale in slumber sleeping
I my loved ones' watch am keeping,
All through the night

Ethan had taught her the lullaby just as his mother had sung it to him. Brenna smiled at the thought of her grandmother, Elizabeth, or Gabriel's wife, Isabelle, singing so sweetly to her son. They must have heard him awaken when she hadn't.

Brenna eased opened the door so as not to disturb them, but the empty room left her shivering. No lamp had been lit or curtains drawn to allow the moonlight inside. Panicked, she hurried to Jacob's crib and found him warm, content, and asleep. She searched every dark corner and checked the windows, but no one else was there.

"Brenna?"

She didn't take her eyes off of Jacob. "In here."

Ethan moved up behind her and wrapped his arms around her waist. "Did he wake up?"

She shook her head. "No, but I heard someone singing to him."

"Elizabeth?"

"No. No one else was in here."

Ethan turned her around. "Is everything all right?"

Exasperated, Brenna looked back down at their son. "I'm not crazy or hearing things. At least I don't think I am. Do you remember the tune you taught me right after Jacob was born?"

He nodded. "My mother's lullaby."

"Yes. Do Gabriel and Eliza know it?"

Ethan shrugged. "I imagine so. Is that what you heard?"

"Yes." She laughed. "Perhaps I did just hear it in my head."

"Do you want to bring him into our room for tonight?"

"I don't wish to disturb him." Brenna leaned over and tucked the edges of the blanket around Jacob. "I'm sorry, I didn't mean to wake you. Let's go back to bed."

Brenna followed her husband into the dark hall but not without one final study of the nursery. This time, she left the door open all the way.

"You look awful."

Brenna looked up from her morning cup of tea and attempted a smile for Ethan's younger sister, Eliza. A new bride to Brenna's brother, Ramsey Cameron, Eliza was now her sister twice over. When Brenna first arrived in Briarwood more than eighteen months ago, she had stumbled unexpectedly into a family whose bond was deeper than any she'd known since the death of her parents. Brenna studied her sister-in-law's lopsided grin. "You don't. Marriage agrees with you."

Eliza grinned. "I won't argue with truth." She poured herself a cup of coffee and sat down across from Brenna. "You're up early. Didn't sleep well?"

"Something kept me awake."

"Ethan?"

Brenna tossed a napkin at Eliza. "Where your thoughts drift is remarkable." Her smile was fleeting. "I thought I heard a woman singing to Jacob, but when I reached his room, no one was there."

Eliza shrugged. "It's probably just the house. She's old and sometimes likes to have her say."

"Perhaps." Brenna drank the rest of her tea and asked, "What are you doing here this early?"

"Elizabeth's attempts to teach me how to cook have gone to waste. I need to place an advertisement for a live-in housekeeper and cook, for Ramsey's sake, and thought I'd stop in first. I never realized how much work Amanda and Elizabeth did, and Mabel before them, until I wasn't living here."

Brenna thought of the grandmother she first met not long after her arrival in Briarwood, Montana. Now, she couldn't imagine life at Hawk's Peak without Elizabeth. "Amanda has been a dream, especially since Grandmother refuses to slow down." Brenna studied her sister-in-law. "Elizabeth is going to teach me how to bake her delicious mince pies this afternoon. Care to join us?"

Eliza laughed. "I'd rather be thrown from a wild mustang."

Brenna smiled. "Not in that dress you won't. Not even a riding skirt for your trip to town."

"Tore up my last one yesterday. Caught it on a nail and ripped it clean through, along with some of my leg."

"Nothing serious, I hope."

"Nope. Ramsey cleaned it up."

Brenna grinned. "A task I'm certain you both enjoyed."

A blush rose up Eliza's cheeks. "Always do. Speaking of tasks, I better get to mine. I wanted to ask if anyone needed anything from town."

"You'll save Gabriel a trip. He said something about an order of lumber he had to pick up tomorrow."

Eliza swallowed the last of her coffee. "I'd give him my list, except I haven't been into town for two weeks."

"Or here in a week. We miss you around here."

"I'll admit, it's strange not to be here every day. The house isn't far, but Ramsey and I have been talking about putting up a cabin nearby." Eliza stretched the muscles in her shoulders against the back of the chair.

"You'd give up the other house?"

Eliza shook her head. "Ever since we decided to put the new stables here instead of at our place, Ramsey and I have considered the time we'll spend here. We don't need a lot of space, and we'll keep the big house, for now." Ramsey and Eliza now lived in the expansive ranch house that once belonged to Nathan Hunter, and although the land was now a part of Hawk's Peak, they had yet to call it home.

"I think it's a wonderful idea."

Brenna and Eliza looked toward the door where their other sister-in-law walked in, hand in hand with Andrew, her younger brother. Isabelle came to Montana as a schoolteacher, hoping for a new beginning for her and Andrew. Unbeknownst to Isabelle at the time, the new beginning included an unexpected love between her and Gabriel Gallagher.

Isabelle sat down next to Andrew and said, "We'd love to see you around here more often and not just in a saddle as you pass through."

Eliza sneaked a cookie and winked at Andrew. "You will over the next couple of weeks since we'll be bunking in my old room. Between the extra horses and Gabriel finishing up the new house, we thought we'd be of more use here."

"I couldn't be more pleased, especially with Christmas so close." Brenna added more hot tea to her cup. "Have you decided where you'd like the cabin?"

"There's a spot west of the main house near the trees." Eliza pushed her now empty coffee mug away, her gaze moving to her nephew. "What's wrong, Andrew? You've barely touched your muffin, and I know for a fact that Amanda's muffins are the best in the territory."

Isabelle smoothed a hand over her brother's hair. "He didn't sleep well. Wandered into my and Gabriel's room early this morning."

Brenna watched Isabelle encourage the sleepy boy to sit up

straight at the table. "What kept you up?"

Andrew yawned. "The lady singing."

Brenna fumbled with her teacup.

Isabelle set a cup of milk in front of Andrew. "Are you well, Brenna?"

She nodded, then focused on Andrew. "You heard a lady singing last night?"

"Uh huh. It was pretty."

Brenna looked up at Isabelle. "So you weren't the one in Jacob's room last night?"

"Brenna, I'm sure it's nothing," Eliza said. "Like I said, this old house likes to make noise."

"Yes, I'm sure it's nothing." Brenna pushed away from the table. "I better get Jacob up."

"Can't be coyotes or wolves. They would have killed their share of the chickens."

"I'm telling you, Ethan, something or someone is taking eggs from the coop."

Ethan studied his wife. "What were you doing out in the chicken coop?"

"Fresh air."

Ethan smiled and draped an arm around his wife's waist. "With the chickens?"

Brenna nodded once, sprigs of red hair framing her face. "Does it matter? That's not the only thing strange happening around here."

"What exactly has happened?"

"Someone's been staying in the east line shack."

"Is this about the singing you heard?"

Brenna managed to keep her frustration in check. "No. I'm willing to concede that I might have imagined a woman singing to our son, though Andrew heard it as well, but I am not imagining this. Ben mentioned it this morning when I was outside."

"With the chickens again?"

"Ethan."

He held up his hands and grinned. "The teasing is over."

Brenna smiled and raised up on her toes to kiss him. "You're an exasperating man, Ethan Gallagher."

"You love me anyway."

"Heaven help me, I do."

"Are we interrupting?"

Ethan and Brenna turned when Gabriel and Eliza walked into the room. Ethan's younger siblings brushed the snow from their coats and stepped into the kitchen.

"Always," Ethan said, but Brenna swatted his arm and smiled at the other two.

"Is the coffee hot?" Gabriel blew into his hands and rubbed them together.

"Fresh pot." Brenna filled two mugs full and passed one to each of the newcomers.

Gabriel said, "We have a problem at the line shack."

"How is it you know and I don't?" Ethan asked, ignoring his wife's smug smile.

"I just spoke with Ben." Gabriel refilled his mug. "Thought he saw smoke, but when he went to check, no one was around. He did say someone's been there. Fresh cinders in the stove."

Eliza pulled out a chair and made herself comfortable. "Ramsey swore he heard something out in the barn last night, and he found fresh prints—too small for a man. He went out to look . . . found nothing suspicious."

Ethan glanced at each one of them. "I can understand that with everything we've been through, there's cause for concern, but you're all a mite paranoid. Bad guys don't sing lullabies or only steal eggs."

Eliza glanced over at him. "And you're not paranoid?"

He shook his head. "For the first time in a decade, our family is going to have a normal and quiet Christmas. The fighting is over, and I for one plan to enjoy it." Ethan pulled his wife closer and pressed his hands gently to her middle.

Gabriel slapped his brother's back. "You already got the best gift a man could want."

Eliza grinned. "Another Gallagher. Now there's something to celebrate."

Gabriel moved his empty cup aside. "Speaking of celebrating, I think we ought to have a holiday gathering."

Brenna's bright smile lit up her green eyes. "What a lovely idea, Gabriel."

Skeptical, Eliza stood and carried her cup to the sink. "Lovely indeed." She turned to her brother. "Since when do you like parties?"

"Dear sister, you're the one who doesn't like them. I, however, will enjoy any chance I get to dance with my wife."

Ethan shrugged. "It's a good idea, although we can't ask people to ride out here in the snow, Gabe."

"We can celebrate in town. I think it's time for everyone to enjoy a fine Christmas. Do you remember the last time Briarwood celebrated the holiday with the entire town?"

Ethan smiled, a faraway look in his eyes. "Not since Mother and Father were around."

Brenna looped her arm with Ethan's. "I'll work with Amanda and Elizabeth. Perhaps we can meet with some of the women in town and plan the details." She gazed up at her husband. "I've not enjoyed a true Christmas celebration since I left Scotland."

Ethan brushed a finger over Brenna's lips and gently squeezed her hand. "You have to promise to take it easy." He leaned closer and lowered his voice. "You've not been feeling well these past few days."

Surprised, she met his eyes. "I didn't realize you'd noticed. I've already born you a child, Ethan Gallagher. I can manage, and I know my limits. My guardian angels have kept a close watch ever since I shared the news."

Eliza glanced around the kitchen. "Speaking of Amanda and your grandmother, where are they?"

"Oh, here and there." Brenna swung a white towel through the air. "They won't allow me to do anything more than stir soup or read a book when Jacob is asleep. I'm going mad." Brenna's thoughts drifted to the older couple who had helped raise her and still looked after Cameron Manor in her absence. "Iain and Maggie hovered just as much when I was in Scotland, pregnant with Jacob."

Gabriel cupped his sister-in-law's face. "You're not going mad, but you are going to have another baby." He grinned up at his brother. "This is going to be a Christmas to remember."

"Not if we don't get our work done around here," Ethan interjected, though he winked at his wife before turning to his sister. "I have a few ideas for the spring stable expansion I'd like to run by you and Ramsey."

Eliza sneaked a sample of the unfrosted cake someone had left on the counter. "I'm headed over to meet Ramsey right now. We have a mare who took a tumble a few days ago."

"Is it serious?" Gabriel asked.

Eliza shook her head. "Ramsey knows what he's doing, but she's one of the mares for the new breeding stock, and he doesn't want to takes any chances. Ethan, if you're ready, we can head over now."

"Let's go, then." Ethan brushed a kiss over Brenna's lips, kissed his son's forehead, and headed outside with Eliza and Gabriel.

They covered the distance between the main house and the

old Hunter spread—Ethan wondered if they'd ever stop thinking of it as Nathan Hunter's house. Two of the men Ramsey employed had cleared a crude path between the two ranches using the horse-drawn wedge plow. The rest of the snow in many areas was flattened by the cattle during the daily rotations for winter grazing and feeding. It made travel between the two properties easier, but not ideal.

When they rode up to the barn, Ethan remembered the day he first brought Brenna to meet her grandfather. Brenna remained strong that day despite Nathan Hunter's cruelty, but it had also been the day Ethan fell in love with Brenna, and that was a memory worth keeping. Ethan refocused when Ramsey stepped out of the barn.

Eliza dismounted and joined her husband. "How's the mare?"

"The leg doesn't appear to be damaged. She's standing on it now." Ramsey kissed his wife and then shook hands with Ethan and Gabriel when they joined them. "Good to see you both. I don't get over to Hawk's Peak as much as I'd like these days."

They followed Ramsey back into the barn and out of the wind. Ethan walked to the stall where the injured mare stood, her head over the stall door. "You've done a good job around this place, though I, too, have to admit we wouldn't mind seeing you around the house more often. Besides, this is a part of Hawk's Peak now."

Ramsey grinned and looked at his wife who said, "We wanted to speak with both of you. Ramsey and I have talked about building a cabin nearby, on the west side of the main house close to the trees. Neither of you would mind, would you?"

Ethan grinned. "Mind? Of course not. It's your land, too."

Gabriel asked, "Why only a cabin? Will you still keep Hunter's . . . I'd better stop calling it that."

"Yes, we'd still keep this ranch house for now, but we'd have a place close by. I wasn't going to say anything . . . as nice as this place is, it still has a feeling of Hunter around it. Ramsey and I want to tear down the old house and start new, make a place that's ours and not something Hunter built. Did you know Elizabeth won't come and visit? We don't press her for a reason, or bring it up, but we know it's because of the unhappy memories."

Ethan draped an arm over Eliza's shoulders. "We can clear land and start on the new cabin after Christmas." He pressed his lips to her forehead in a brief kiss and then ruffled her messy hair, knowing it would bring out a smile."

She swatted his hand away and leaned into Ramsey.

Ramsey said, "I'd like to be the one to tell Elizabeth and make sure she's in agreement. It's one thing not to want to visit, but another knowing the place is gone for good."

"We won't say anything, and I'll ask Brenna to keep your plans quiet as well."

"Appreciate it." Ramsey checked the mare once more before they left the barn.

Gabriel stopped, turned a full circle, and asked, "Where are the men you hired?"

"Gone." Ramsey secured the barn doors and slipped an arm around Eliza's waist. "One of them took off and the other I had to fire. He spent more time with a bottle than working. You take it for granted, but good help is hard to find. Most of your men have been with you for years, and they're loyal. As you've reminded me, this is a part of Hawk's Peak now, and the men who work here should be as loyal."

Ethan said, "Work's always a tad slower in the winter, so if you need some extra help around here, let me know. I'm sure the men would be happy to come over."

"I'd be grateful, though it's helped since we've combined the herds. Eliza and I can manage the horses until we get the next phase of the stables completed."

"I wanted to talk to you about that," Ethan began.

He shared his ideas for the new expansion as the small group walked into the house. Ramsey and Eliza, in turn, shared their thoughts about what would be best for the animals. When they'd finished their second cup of coffee, Ethan and Gabriel said their goodbyes and headed back to the main house.

Ben met up with them halfway home.

"Something wrong?" Ethan asked.

"We have a visitor." Ben brushed his gloved hand across his brow and replaced his hat. "On a hunch, I left a few things out at the line shack in the north pasture the other day, and sure enough, the blanket was used and the food eaten."

"Drifter? Trapper, maybe?" Ethan scanned the open land between the ranch and the tree line. The shack was too far out to see, but there was no mistaking the gentle curls of smoke rising from the chimney pipe. "They haven't gone after the cattle."

Ben shook his head. "I can't see that they've done anything more than steal a few eggs."

"Eliza said Ramsey heard something out at their place."

Ben nodded. "You want me and the boys to take shifts and catch the fella?"

"Not yet." Ethan shifted in the saddle and looked to Gabriel. "The winter was off to a cold start, and it's not getting better. Last night was one of the coldest in memory." Ethan bit down on a piece of jerky. "On second thought, let's go have a look now ourselves."

Catie patted the low flames with the pan in an effort to extinguish the fire but only served to ignite it further. Panicking, she left the fire burning, and stumbled from the shack. She raced toward the trees, and once she was safely beneath her canopy of pines, she realized her scarf still lay on the bed.

She huddled between two large pines, remaining low to the ground with the hope that the needled branches would hide her from view. Her hope did not last long.

"Not what I expected."

Catie slowly rose and turned around. She had not heard the man approach from behind.

"Do you have a name, young lady?"

She debated answering him. She was not keen on going to jail for trespassing, nor could she outrun him.

"Catherine Rose Carr, but I'm called Catie." She watched his warm blue eyes study her and realized his presence offered her more comfort than fear.

"Well, Catie, I suppose you're the one who's been sleeping in our range shack."

She nodded and stepped back when the man began to remove his coat. He stopped.

"You're scared, but it's cold out, and you can't remain here on your own. You don't need to fear me."

"That's what bad men say."

He chuckled and finished removing his coat. "You don't have to take my word for it. While you're sorting out whether you can trust me, take this." He handed her the coat.

Unwilling to freeze, but still wary, Catie accepted the large garment and slipped her arms into the sleeves. The heavy coat smelled of horses.

"Thank you," she mumbled. "Don't go thinking we're friends now."

"I wouldn't dare, but you'll still have to come with me. We need to talk, and I'd rather not stay out here in the cold. I know my wife would like you to meet you."

"What's your name, mister?"

He tipped his hat. "Ethan Gallagher. I believe you're acquainted with our chicken coop."

She had the courtesy to blush. "I reckon I'll go." Catie paused and narrowed her eyes. "You wouldn't be trying anything funny, would you?"

Ethan grinned and held up his hands in defense. "On my honor, I am not."

3

Catie stared wide-eyed at the sprawling ranch house. Her gaze darted from one building to the next and over the snow-covered pastures where men rode among a herd large enough to feed an entire town. She'd seen the spread glimpses during her foray to the chicken coop, but fear had kept her from indulging in further examination of the property. It looked bigger now, more imposing.

"What is this place?"

"Hawk's Peak."

Catie accepted Ethan's help off the back of his horse. Still wrapped up in his warm coat, she followed him to the front porch, then stopped. "I'm not so sure about this."

"Listen, I don't know your story, or why you were hiding in the shack, but it's no place for a person to live. We'll get to the telling part. Right now you need a hot meal and a warm bed." Ethan gestured to the front door. "You can come inside now, or I can take you into town and turn you over to the reverend until we can find your family. Either way, you're not going back out there."

Catie considered her options, but it was something her father used to say that made the decision. He used to tell her a fool is a person who didn't recognize something good when it happened to them. Joseph Carr didn't raise a fool.

"Why are you helping me, Mr. Gallagher?"

He didn't answer her question. Instead he smiled and walked to the door. Curious about the man, and with a strong need for the hot meal he promised, Catie stepped into the house.

An older woman with touches of gray woven into her dark hair, walked toward them.

"I see you've brought us a guest."

Ethan lowered his strong hand to her shoulder, and Catie relaxed.

"A guest in need of one of your delicious meals. Catie, this is Elizabeth, my grandmother, or my wife's grandmother to be precise."

Catie looked up at him, a question of concern and defiance in her eyes. "Can I trust her?"

Ethan smiled back down at her. "With your life. She also happens to be one of the best cooks in Montana."

Catie watched Elizabeth and Ethan exchange a look she couldn't interpret and might have given more careful study to if the scent of home cooking hadn't distracted her. She nodded, offering no verbal agreement. Her near-empty stomach did most of the talking.

Ethan asked Elizabeth, "Is Brenna down here?"

"She's upstairs with Jacob. I told her to rest, but you know her." Elizabeth turned to Catie. "I have fresh corn bread hot from the oven and soup on the stove. I might even have a slice of apple pie left."

Elizabeth made no attempt to touch Catie. She wouldn't have minded, but Catie felt unkempt standing beside the woman. She gave Ethan one more quick study before she slipped out of his coat and did her best to smile. There hadn't been many reasons to smile lately. "Thank you, Mr. Gallagher. I reckon you aren't all bad." Without another word, she allowed Elizabeth to guide her into the kitchen.

Catie washed her hands in a basin with an earthy scented soap and reached for the clean white cloth Elizabeth set out for her. The fabric was soft against her skin and smelled faintly of fresh air. The quick cleaning of her hands served as a further reminder that she was covered in days-worth of filth.

"Come and sit down right here, child." Elizabeth tapped the back of a chair.

Catie watched Elizabeth place a bowl of thick soup and three pieces of corn bread on the table. The raw ache of emptiness in her stomach worsened. She paced herself for three bites, then hunger took priority over manners. Broth overflowed the spoon and spilled back into the bowl. She held the spoon mid-air and glanced around the room. Elizabeth had moved from the stove to sit at the table. A deep blush heated her cheeks and warmed her skin before she put the spoon down and tucked her hands onto her lap.

"I'm sorry, ma'am."

Catie didn't expect the warm smile that appeared without hesitation on the woman's face.

"Please call me, Elizabeth. One might conjecture that I'm old enough to be called 'ma'am,' but I don't feel a day older than . . . well, never you mind. I like to see someone who appreciates my cooking. Would you like some more?"

Catie looked down at her nearly empty bowl and the few crumbs left on the small plate. She didn't know what to say. Elizabeth seemed to know what she needed because she scooped another serving of soup into the bowl and added another slice of warm corn bread to the plate. Catie thanked her and managed to eat unhurried this time.

Elizabeth left her alone to enjoy the meal, yet remained in the kitchen, humming a soft tune. Catie didn't recognize the peaceful melody, and the stiffness left her shoulders while she listened to the sweet sound. Her eyes drifted close, then quickly opened when she heard the sound of heavy footsteps in the hall.

A looming frame filled the doorway. Catie tensed, then relaxed when her eyes focused. The man looked like Ethan.

Elizabeth turned away from the stove, her big smile lighting up her eyes. "Where have you been, Gabriel? We expected you more than an hour ago."

He stepped inside the kitchen. Catie noticed his gaze touched briefly on her, but he seemed not to give her much thought.

"Otis took a fall while we were loading the lumber."

"He wasn't injured too badly, I hope."

"Nothing some of Doc Brody's ointment won't fix." Catie watched Gabriel lean against a door frame by the stove and focus his attention on her.

"The name is Gabriel."

His smile was as warm and kind as Ethan's. The blue in his eyes brightened when he grinned, and Catie figured they must be kin. She remembered what it was like to have kin.

"My name is Catherine Rose Carr, but people just call me Catie."

"Glad to meet you, *just* Catie." Gabriel pushed away from the door, sneaked two muffins from the pan Elizabeth pulled out of the oven, and tossed one to her. Surprised, Catie caught it. She dropped the hot muffin down on the plate and grinned up at him. He settled into the chair opposite her and bit down into the warm muffin.

"Best cook around."

"Flattery doesn't work on me, Gabriel Gallagher."

Gabriel winked at Catie and said to Elizabeth, "Does this mean we don't get your sweet peach dumpling for Christmas dessert?"

Elizabeth swatted Gabriel lightly with the edge of a towel, but Catie saw the pink hue on the woman's round cheeks. To Catie, it looked like love.

Gabriel turned his attention back to her. "Who'd you come home with, Catie Rose?"

"Me."

Everyone looked to the doorway where Ethan now stood, his arms wrapped around a small woman with thick hair the color of a sunrise. Catie could see the reds dance across the early morning sky before she blinked and saw the woman was just a person. She couldn't explain what happened in that moment, except she knew the tears filling her eyes were real. Catie swiped at them and breathed deeply. The woman kissed and hugged Gabriel and Elizabeth, then made her way to the table. When Ethan's wife sat down next to her, Catie's first instinct was to pull away. She didn't want her stink and dirty clothes to offend her, but the lady didn't seem to mind.

"Catie, this is my wife, Brenna."

Brenna smiled and faced her. "Ethan's told me you've come to stay with us awhile."

Catie looked past Brenna to Ethan to find him smiling.

"I don't know, Mrs. Gallagher. I'm grateful for the food, but I can't—"

"Of course you can," Elizabeth said from the other side of the kitchen. She didn't bother to turn around.

"Call me Brenna." Brenna leaned closer. "Elizabeth is right. You'll need a few days to rest at least. Please let us help you."

Catie glanced from Gabriel to Ethan, then back to Brenna. "I don't know if you can."

Gabriel leaned back in his chair. "It can't hurt to try, can it?"

Catie looked up once more at Ethan. Something in the way he looked at her, like she wished her father would have, told her that if she trusted him, everything would be all right. Catie desperately wanted to believe him.

"I don't know."

Brenna drew Catie's focus once more. "How about a trade instead?"

Catie's right eyebrow rose up. "What kind of trade?"

"Can you cook?" Elizabeth had joined them.

Catie shook her head. "I can sew and hunt."

Brenna stared at her in surprise. It was a reaction Catie had grown accustomed to over the years.

"There's plenty of sewing and small chores around the house. Do you like children younger than you?"

Catie nodded. "At least, I think I do. I don't reckon I know much about them."

"I have a son who is less than two years. He might enjoy someone else's company. So, do you agree to the trade?"

Catie looked skeptical. "You want me to help sew and look after your son, and I get to stay here?" She remembered what the house looked like from the outside. "It's not a fair trade. I got to earn my keep or I can't stay."

Ethan stepped forward then. "Work around here can be tough. I promise you'll earn your keep."

A warm fire at night and a clean bed. A roof that didn't leak the rain and let in the cold. She had dreamt of this kind of life, not knowing how long it might last. Nothing good for her lasted long. If she stayed, she could try Elizabeth's peach dumpling Gabriel talked about.

Catie nodded once. "Where do I start?"

4

Ethan woke from a rare night of deep slumber. His wife lay curled up next to him under the heavy quilts. He heard the creak of the floorboards in the hall again. On bare feet, and without a shirt, he walked across the room to open the door. On the other side was a dark and empty hallway. No sounds came from the other end of the hall or from Jacob's nursery.

Annoyed with himself for succumbing to Brenna's worries about hearing someone in their son's room, Ethan grabbed the shirt he'd discarded before bed and made his way to the room next door. Jacob slept peacefully, just as he had the night before. The rocker in the corner swayed softly, but his own movements into the room could have caused that.

Assured his son was safe, Ethan left the door open and returned to the hall. He heard the creak again. A soft light shined downstairs. Careful to stay on the rugs and carpets so as not to wake anyone, Ethan walked down the stairs and through the halls to the study door. It was closed and a bright light seeped from underneath. His hand turned the knob and inched the door open, only, he wasn't quick enough.

"Son of a—"

Gabriel's smiling face waited on the other side of the threshold. "Thought I heard someone out here."

Ethan exhaled and pushed into the study, closing the door behind him. "What in the hell are you doing down here this late?"

Gabriel laughed. "Is my big brother checking on me?"

"No. I heard someone upstairs and then saw the light down here."

Gabriel sobered. "You must be hearing things, too. I've been down here for an hour."

Ethan rubbed a hand over his face. "You weren't just walking around up in the hall?"

"Sorry, brother, but you are hearing things." Gabriel walked to the desk where it appeared he'd been working.

"What are you doing down here?"

Gabriel motioned Ethan over. "I'm putting some finishing touches on a couple of surprises to the house for Isabelle. Otis is helping me out—he has a real eye for the details—and I promised I'd have the rest of the plans to him by tomorrow."

"At this rate, Otis will be able to give up his blacksmith shop to build for us full-time." Ethan settled in next to his brother and studied the drawing. "You've expanded."

Gabriel nodded. "Isabelle wants children, and so do I."

"It hasn't been that long."

"I know, but I want Isabelle to know I'm planning ahead."

Ethan studied the plans again. "For a lot, I see." He grinned. "You're already two ahead of us."

Two children. Ethan had believed it would be Gabriel to become a father first. He continued to smile and study the plans. His brother's new home was a slightly updated, though somewhat smaller, version of the main ranch house. Ethan liked knowing he'd be able to look out the window and see his brother's home. He felt more comfortable having at least one other sibling within shouting distance. They may have found peace with the recent passing of Nathan Hunter, but the land was still wild, and some of the men on it even more so.

Peace. Ethan almost couldn't believe it. When he'd found Brenna more than a year ago, he thought he'd been given a gift he hadn't deserved. Then Jacob came along and changed their lives for the better. When Brenna's brother, Ramsey, returned to Montana after nearly a decade away, the Gallaghers put an end to the destruction Nathan Hunter had brought into their lives and into their parents' lives. Ramsey took his true father's name of Cameron and left the Hunter chapter of his life behind. Now the Gallaghers could watch their family grow without the worry and hatred they'd dealt with while Hunter lived.

"It looks good. Isabelle's going to be pleased."

Gabriel rolled up the plans and set them aside. "I know you and Brenna offered us a place here, and there's plenty of room, but I want Isabelle to have a home of her own."

"I get it, brother, I do. I'd want the same for Brenna, though I think she'll miss having Isabelle around."

Gabriel laughed. "There are still plenty of females here. Speaking of which, have you learned anything more about Catie?"

"She's not volunteering much."

"Can't blame her. She's been on her own, and we can't know for how long. She's a tough one."

Ethan smiled and looked at his brother. "I like the kid."

"I like her, too. I told Andrew about her, and he asked if she would play with him."

"I imagine Catie would be willing. She's eager for companionship, even if she won't admit it." Ethan considered and then asked, "Did you have a chance to speak with Ramsey?"

Gabriel crossed his arms and sat on the edge of the desk. "I did. He said he knows enough sheriffs and deputies in Montana and Wyoming, so he'd ask around. You ever hear of someone named Carr in these parts?"

"No, but the area is changing. A lot of drifters coming through here."

"The problem is, the kid doesn't look or sound like she was raised by a drifter."

"No, she doesn't. I'm hoping Brenna will have some luck getting through to her." Ethan nodded toward the door, then quieted when it inched opened.

Eliza stood in the threshold wearing a thick, white nightgown and the heavy robe she favored in the winter. It appeared she'd been deep in sleep by her weary eyes.

"We ought to have a system for announcing ourselves. Is everything all right, Eliza?"

She nodded on a yawn. "I remember now why Ramsey and I moved out. Quiet." She walked on bare feet into the room and stood in front of the desk. "Your wives have more sense than the two of you. What are you doing awake?"

Ethan shrugged. "I thought I heard something, but it turned out to be Gabriel." He studied his sister's rumbled appearance and quirked a brow. "Didn't you and Ramsey go to bed only an hour ago?"

"Yes, and I'd like to be back there, but you two clods woke me up."

Gabriel held up his hands in defense. "It wasn't me. I've been downstairs since you went to bed."

"I'm headed back up now." He glanced at his brother. "You're sure you weren't the one up in the hall?"

Gabriel picked up the lamp from the table and followed his brother and sister from the study. "Wasn't me. Speaking of strange things, does anyone know how to play the piano yet?"

"Isabelle's teaching Brenna. Why?"

"Could have sworn I heard it earlier before I came downstairs."

Ethan laughed quietly as they climbed the stairs. "Now who's imagining things?"

5

Catie woke in a panic until she realized the blankets covering her were on a clean bed and the windows that looked out to the morning sun fit securely in their wood frames. Her breathing steadied, and she pushed her loose brown curls away from her eyes. The night before, she'd experienced her first hot bath in months. Her long braids had not come undone easily, but Brenna had patiently helped her loosen and brush the long strands until they shone.

Secretly, she was grateful.

She didn't remember her mother, and her father had refused to talk about the woman who'd left them behind when Catie was figuring out how to walk on the two feet God gave her. She still had no answers, but on this morning she felt safer than she had in years.

Better not to put too much thought into it. Before long, she'd make her way back to another abandoned cabin and hide away until her pa came for her. Then again, Catie wasn't certain she wanted him to come back. The fear of having to fend for herself outweighed the fear of not knowing who to can trust and depend upon.

Anxious to start on whatever chores they had planned for her, Catie pushed back the blankets and climbed down from the bed.

She allowed herself a moment to enjoy the sensation of a thick rug beneath her feet. She wiggled her bare toes, and then walked to the window. A snowy landscape dotted with trees and cattle greeted her. She spotted a few men already on horseback and wondered if the chores might require her to ride one of the beautiful animals.

She padded back over to the bed and stared down at the small pile of folded clothes on the trunk. Her clothes. Catie lifted the dress on top and smoothed her hand over the worn fabric, now clean and free of dirt and stench. She sat beside the clothes on the trunk and gave the room a careful study. It was a life that didn't belong to her. She ate at their table, slept in their bed, and would earn her keep until they decided what to do with her, but the truth still remained—this life wasn't hers.

Catie swiped at the single tear as it slid down her cheek. She splashed cold water on her face from a porcelain bowl and peeked at herself in the clean mirror above the washstand.

"You can do this, Catie Rose."

She tidied the room the best she knew how, and with one more deep breath, she went in search of a Gallagher.

The upstairs was quiet despite the early hour. When Catie descended the stairs, she heard a low mingling of voices and laughter. Scents of breakfast and baking wafted from down the hall, drawing her to the kitchen. She stopped at the threshold and hugged her body against the wall just outside. She stood witness to a family, and an intimate longing filled her heart.

Elizabeth bustled around the stove with a younger woman who Catie hadn't seen the day before. She laughed at something Elizabeth said and pounded a fist into a large round ball of dough. A third woman, tall and fair, sat beside a young boy at the table who smiled in between bites of breakfast. Brenna, the beautiful wife of Ethan, watched over a baby tucked safely in a basket on the table while she peeled potatoes. The scene reminded her of the March family in *Little Women*, what she imagined a family looked like.

"Good morning, Catie."

Catie turned her head quickly to look at Elizabeth. The woman's smile warmed the cold around her heart much as it had the day before.

"You won't have much luck eating breakfast if you don't come in." Elizabeth motioned to the table, and with five pairs of eyes focused on her, Catie entered, but didn't sit.

"Can I help?"

"You eat first."

The fair-haired woman continued to look at her when Catie sat down across from her and the boy.

"Are you sad?"

Catie looked at the boy, then forced a smile for his benefit. "No."

The woman leaned down and spoke quietly to the boy before turning back to Catie. "My name is Isabelle, and this is my brother, Andrew. He's curious and filled with questions."

Catie nodded. "Nice to meet you." Even to her own ears the words sounded forced. She struggled against the instinct to turn into herself and shut out everyone and everything. The woman's kindness and the young boy's curious eyes calmed Catie's anxiety a little. She knew they weren't going to hurt her or say things to her that might bruise her spirit.

Brenna finished peeling potatoes and set aside the odd tool she'd been using. Catie watched her with her own cautious curiosity even as she observed the others in the room. Isabelle nodded once, her eyes on Brenna, before she told her brother he could play upstairs before his lessons. The boy whooped in excitement, thanked Elizabeth for breakfast, and started to run from the room. He careened to a halt at the doorway and turned. "I was sad when I came here, too, but they'll make it better."

Andrew dashed from the room, leaving his words behind.

Catie watched the others, all quiet now. Brenna broke the silence first. "After breakfast, why don't we go for a walk?"

Catie glanced toward the window.

"I know, it's cold and snowing, but we won't go far. The fresh air will do us both some good."

Catie thought how much Brenna enjoyed her fresh air. She remembered what Brenna had told the other lady in chicken coop about getting fresh air and gathering pinecones. She smiled, nodded, and said, "I'd like that."

A pretty woman with hair the same color as the oats she used to feed her pa's horse, set a plate of food on the table in front of Catie. "I'm Amanda, and I hope you like eggs. Elizabeth makes the biscuits from a special recipe she won't share with anyone." Amanda winked. Catie returned her smile and thanked her for the food.

Once Catie had her fill of fried eggs, biscuits, and sausages, she offered to clean the kitchen and help with the house chores. Instead, Brenna coaxed her from the kitchen, handed her a coat that must have belonged to one of the women, and guided her out the front door. Catie wasn't used to being guided anywhere. She didn't have long to wait before she understood why Brenna wanted to speak with her alone.

"Ramsey, my brother, and Ethan, came across a cabin yesterday west of here. It appears some men have been occupying it for a few days, but they found some items . . ."

Catie's body stiffened. She knew those "items" belonged to her. There wasn't much, but it had been hers.

Brenna continued. "Were you living there, Catie?"

Catie refused to hang her head in shame. "Yes, but my pa was coming back. He just had to find work." The cold worked its way over her face and through the worn leather of her boots, but the coat kept her warmer than she'd been in many winters.

"Was the cabin yours and your father's?"

This time Catie shrugged. She didn't know anything, and who could say something belonged to one person if it could be so easily taken away. "I can take care of myself. I don't want to go to any church or to some city to live with other kids."

Brenna stopped near the barn, forcing Catie to stop with her. "We wouldn't send you away."

"I figured you'd send me to a church man to go with . . ." Catie hated even the thought of the word, ". . . orphans."

"Are you an orphan, Catie?" Brenna framed the girl's face with her hands. "Is your father coming back?"

"He said so."

"Then you'll stay here until he does."

6

Catie peeked around the corner before walking into the kitchen. She had thought a lot about what Brenna said, but she didn't want to hope for a life she couldn't have. Her pa would return, and she'd have to leave the ranch—and the Gallaghers.

"Looking for someone?"

Catie cringed and stood straight. She'd been caught sneaking around their house, except Ethan didn't look upset. He was smiling, and Catie found herself returning the smile with unexpected ease.

"Not really."

Ethan looked like he'd just come in from outside. Catie didn't know how she missed hearing the door open. Two days at the ranch, and she was already careless.

"Have you ever ridden a horse, Catie?"

She wanted to, but her pa only ever had one horse, and she wasn't allowed to ride him. She shook her head.

"Want a lesson? We have a gentle mare in the stable. Andrew learned to ride on her."

Catie didn't have a chance to be embarrassed that a young boy knew how to ride and she couldn't. Any possible embarrassment paled next to her desire to learn.

"You don't mind?"

Ethan chuckled. "Not a bit. I have to make my rounds of the pastures, and I wouldn't mind some company."

Her eyes widened. "I can't ride that far, can I?"

"There are no limits here." Ethan looked her up and down. Catie wondered if he noticed she wore the same dress as the day before or if her boots were too worn to stand much time in the cold. He appeared to see everything. Catie watched his eyes brighten and his smile widen. She turned around to see Brenna coming down the stairs, holding her son.

"You're a sight, Ethan Gallagher." Brenna approached them and surprised Catie by handing over a curious Jacob. "Have you ever held a baby, Catie?"

Catie shook her head. "What if I drop him?"

Brenna smiled. "You're doing fine, and Jacob is already taken with you. Are you going back out?"

Ethan nodded. "Thought I'd take Catie for a riding lesson and show her a bit of the ranch."

"A wonderful idea." Brenna scooped Jacob out of Catie's arms and passed him to Ethan. "She'll need something proper to wear. Come with me, Catie."

Brenna grasped her hand and pulled her toward the stairs. Catie looked back at Ethan who shrugged, grinned, and started talking to his son.

Catie stopped at the threshold of Brenna's bedroom, a little in awe at the simple beauty. She'd never seen anything so fine as the Gallagher's home, and she imagined by the time she got used to it, she'd have to leave.

Brenna rummaged through her bureau and pulled out an outfit too fine for Catie to wear.

She shook her head and backed up. "I can't."

"Of course you can. We'll have to belt it for today, but then we can alter it, or Elizabeth can. I regret to say I'm not as skilled with a needle as I'd like."

Catie ran her fingers over the dark blue wool. "I can sew."

Brenna looked up from the riding habit. "You said as much. And hunt, too. With what?"

Catie shrugged. "My pa taught me to shoot and skin what I killed."

Brenna didn't look at her strangely or tell her that hunting and skinning weren't ladylike. What she did say surprised Catie. "I'll be sure to introduce you to Eliza, Ethan's sister. She's not one for domestic life, but she can ride and shoot as well, or perhaps better, than most men on this ranch."

Wide-eyed, Catie momentarily forgot about the beautiful riding clothes. "Really?"

"And truly. You'll like Eliza." Brenna handed her the outfit and motioned to a screen in the corner. "Change into this, and I'll find a pair of boots for you. How old are you, Catie?"

Catie asked herself that same question every winter and shrugged. "Fourteen, I think." Catie thought she saw Brenna's eyes darken and her smile disappear, but she might have imagined it.

"Your feet don't look much smaller than mine. I'll see what I have that might fit." Brenna produced a pair of black leather boots with laces up the front and a pair of woolen socks. Catie slipped her feet into the boots and found they almost fit. When they stepped outside, the cold didn't penetrate the borrowed boots like they had her worn shoes.

Catie stood beneath the gray sky in Brenna's riding clothes. The blue velvet was cinched at the waist, but she was tall and the hem didn't reach past her ankles. She watched the white mare toss her head. If Catie didn't believe better, she'd swear the mare smiled at her.

"Are you sure I can do this?"

Brenna leaned in and placed a comforting arm on her shoulder. "I remember my first time on a horse. I was younger than you and terrified. Once I got on, my father couldn't keep me away. You'll do just fine."

Catie remained silent. Climbing onto the pretty mare would be simple. Her problem would come when she wouldn't want to get off. The moment was like a dream, and she didn't want it to end.

Comfortable in the saddle, Catie accepted the reins from Brenna who stood beside her with an encouraging smile. Ethan sat atop a tall black stallion. His black hat didn't cover all the thick hair beneath, and some of it curled around his neck and ears. The big shearling he wore looked like it had seen a dozen winters and could last a dozen more. Ethan and Gabriel looked nothing like her father or most of the men she'd seen with her father over the years.

"You ready?"

Catie glanced at Ethan before nodding. "I don't know what to do."

"Hold onto the reins like this," Ethan demonstrated, "and don't pull too tight. Give her some room and she'll follow. If you want to stop, just pull back a little. If you want to move forward, squeeze your heels against her, but not too much. She likes a gentle touch and won't do you wrong. If you get scared, just let me know."

"Enjoy yourself." Smiling, Brenna patted her leg and moved away. As Ethan passed, Catie watched him lean down low from the horse's back and kiss his wife.

She followed Ethan, or better yet, her mare followed his stallion, over the snowy pastures. They rode along the fences and counted heads of cattle. She met three of the ranch hands who were on shift that morning. One of them looked a little like her pa and smiled like him, too. The cold air fought with her lungs, but she liked it—enjoyed feeling alive.

Ethan motioned her forward and pointed north to south.

"There used to be a fence running along this side of our land. It separated Hawk's Peak from the neighboring ranch."

"What happened to it?"

"It belonged to Brenna's grandfather, but it's all part of Hawk's Peak now."

Catie stared in awe at the expanse of land. "This is all yours?"

Ethan chuckled. "My father used to say we only borrow the land. We harvest it, our cattle graze and rest on it, and the land offers us food, wood for our homes and hearths, and herds for us to hunt."

Catie thought she understood what he was saying, but he said things in a way her own father never did. "What do you mean borrow the land? Don't you own it?"

Ethan leaned over his saddle horn. "Technically, our father bought the land and built the ranch, and our names are on the deed, but one day the land will pass to the next generation, and they'll have it only for their lifetimes, and then their children will borrow it after them for generations."

Catie considered Ethan's words. "My pa told me a person ain't worth much if they don't own land. Do you believe that?"

"I believe owning land, a home, or anything you've worked hard for, and struggled for, makes a man feel like he's worth something, and that he's made his mark on life. There's value in the simple day-to-day living, but to truly have a sense of owning something, you must first know you are a worthy person here." Ethan tapped his chest near his heart. "Let's head back in. It'll be time for lunch, and you must be cold. I sure could use a warm fire about now."

Catie shrugged. "Not too cold anymore. I like riding. I like the freedom and that fresh air Brenna likes so much."

Ethan smiled at her. "It's a nice feeling." He turned his horse back around toward the house. "Now, why don't we try . . ."

Catie watched his face change in an instant. His blue eyes

became sharper, his mouth tighter. His body stiffened, and he held up a hand to keep her from talking. Her father used to do the same thing when they were hiding and he didn't want to be found.

"Catie, I want you to stay close and keep calm." She watched him pull a gun from his belt. "You said you hunt. Have you ever shot a pistol?"

She nodded. "Lots of times."

"We'll test your skills later, but right now take this." Ethan handed her his pistol and pulled a rifle out of the leather scabbard. "I want you to walk the mare, not run, and stay by my side. We're going to go back to the ranch. Keep your eyes forward and the gun close to you."

Catie's hand shook but not enough to release her tight grip on the gun. "What's wrong?"

"We have company, and not the social kind."

Ethan moved his horse forward, and Catie did the same. She rode close enough so that her leg sometimes brushed against Ethan's stallion. She'd managed to get out of some tough situations but nothing that required a gun. She liked the weight of the Colt in her hand. It rested on her lap, ready in case she had to lift and shoot.

She saw the visitors. Three men. They moved to the east, which put them on her left. Ethan was on her right.

"Catie, I need you to look forward okay?"

She nodded. "Who are they?"

"Can't tell from this far off, but they're closing in fast. We're not far from the ranch, so they must not know where we are."

Catie couldn't help but look when Ethan swore. It was a word she didn't know except her father said it a few times when something bad happened.

"How do you feel on the horse?"

Catie remained silent.

"Catie. Can you ride by yourself?"

She looked down at the mare, steady and sure beneath the saddle and seemingly unperturbed by the impending danger. "I don't know."

"That's okay." Ethan reached out and placed her hands on the saddle horn. He then tied a loose knot with the edges of the leather reins and slipped the loop over the saddle, with enough give for the mare to move freely. "Don't let go of the horn, keep your heels pointed down, and don't look back. Can you do that for me?"

Catie gritted her teeth and swiped at the tears falling down her cheek. She nodded. "I promise."

"Good girl. You won't have far to ride, but don't stop. One of the men will see you coming and help."

She nodded again and held on tight. Ethan slapped the rump of the horse and fired off a shot from his rifle.

Ethan waited only a second, trusting the mare to return home on her own. The three visitors made their move, each one rushing forward in different directions. The ranch hands with the cattle would have heard the shot, yet they wouldn't arrive before one of the three reached Catie. Ethan raced forward, riding to block the progress of the man closest to the girl's path. A shot fired, not from his gun, and pierced the snow beside his horse. Another bullet coursed through the air passed Ethan's shoulder; he continued closing in on the attacker.

The other man must have known he wouldn't get away because he swerved, forcing his horse to turn in a wide circle. He fired awkwardly over his shoulder which is why Ethan raised his gun and shot, aiming for the ground in front of the man's horse. The animal reared back, dropping its rider into the snow, then continued on with an empty saddle.

Ethan turned his stallion around to see the other two men in the distance. One retreated back to the trees, and the other was surrounded by three of the men from the ranch. Ethan brought his horse to a stop and patted the stallion's neck before returning to the fallen man who had foolishly attempted to run through the deep, soft-packed snow.

"You won't get far. Best to stop now."

The man did halt and held his hands out wide. Slowly, he turned. Ethan didn't recognize him, but that didn't mean much in a time when strangers had become more prevalent in Montana. With talk of a spur line coming north through Briarwood after the last one was routed southwest, the transient population had increased. Although most passed through town, some remained, hoping to find work at one of the farms or ranches in the area. Others just caused trouble.

Ethan held the rifle on the man and remained on his horse. "Who are you, and what are you doing on my land?"

The man had the decency, or perhaps felt enough fear, to answer. "Looking for someone."

"Your mistake was in coming after me on my own ranch. One of your friends is with my men, and we'll find the other."

The man shook his head, causing his long beard to brush the edge of his tattered coat. "We wasn't after you."

Ethan kept his rifle trained on the man. "The only person with me was a young girl. What business could you have with her? Who are you?"

"Name's Cyrus. We don't want the girl, we want her pa."

Ethan indicated toward the ranch with his rifle. "You're going to walk in, and then you're going to jail."

"Carr owes me money. A lot of money. You can't keep a man from collectin' what's due him."

"No, but I can put him in jail for trespassing on my land and shooting at me. Now move." Ethan followed behind Cyrus as he struggled through the deep snow. They didn't get far before Ben, Hawk's Peak's foreman, rode up with Cyrus's runaway horse. Gabriel was next to him, his rifle ready and in hand.

"The other one didn't make it, Ethan," Gabriel said. "The fool tripped and caught himself with his own knife when Ben tried to disarm him."

Ethan swore and then leaned down over his saddle. "Get on the horse, Cyrus. I'd just as soon get you off my land."

Cyrus reached for the reins. Ben held them back and laughed. "Get on the horse."

Cyrus scowled up at the men, then pulled himself onto the back of his roan gelding. With the rifle still pointed at Cyrus, Gabriel tied the man's hands tightly together and then to the horn. Ben led the horse while Ethan rode beside and slightly to the back and Gabriel rode alongside. It wasn't long before they reached the barn.

Ethan glanced around, not seeing what he wanted. "Where is she?"

"Ethan!"

His head whipped around to the front porch of the house. Catie ran down the steps and across the distance to where he dismounted. She flung herself into his arms, surprising them both. "You okay?"

She nodded against him, and he watched his wife make her way to them.

"I told you he would come home, Catie." Brenna rubbed her hand over the girl's back.

Ethan eased her back, and mindful of their unwanted company, he nodded to his wife who settled her arm over Catie's shoulders and pulled her away. "You did really well, Catie, but right now I need you to go back inside with Brenna."

Catie didn't respond. Her eyes had narrowed and she stared up at Cyrus. Ethan stepped in front of her, blocking Catie's view of him.

"Come on now," Brenna coaxed, except Catie's eyes remained fixated on the stranger.

"Hello, Uncle Cyrus."

7

Catie had experienced hunger and the uncertainty of where she'd sleep or if she would survive a night during a long winter. She knew what it felt like to have her stomach churn until she no longer wanted to breathe. She couldn't explain the vile taste that filled her mouth, but there it was, lodged right beside her disgust.

"Did you kill my pa?"

Cyrus spit on the ground and looked away. "I didn't do nothing to him."

Gabriel gripped the back of Cyrus's collar, leaned close, and whispered to her uncle. Catie wished she knew what Gabriel said because her uncle stopped grumbling."

Catie stepped away from Brenna, and Ethan blocked her from getting too close to a man she hadn't seen in more than five years. Ethan couldn't know that, but Ethan was what her pa called perceptive, though Catie thought her pa didn't know what perceptive meant. "Pa said you were dead."

"Where is my brother?"

Ethan held up his hand to stop her from saying anything else. "Quiet, Cyrus. You can ask any questions you want at the jail, but you won't be talking to her again. Get him out of here, Ben."

Ben nodded. "There's enough light. I'll take the wagon and

get him into town. The other one I'll drop off at Doc Brody's clinic."

Ben rode away, leading Cyrus on his horse behind him. Cyrus shouted about Joseph Carr and his money, but everyone ignored him. Gabriel dismounted and slid his rifle into the leather scabbard attached to his saddle.

Ethan hunched down in front of Catie. "Cyrus is your uncle?"

"Yes."

"Do you know what he wants?"

Catie shrugged. "My pa didn't like him."

"All right." Ethan stood and smoothed a hand over her head, then bent to kiss his wife. "You'll take care of her? Gabe and I need to help Ben get the . . . men loaded into the wagon."

Brenna nodded and managed to draw Catie away. When they entered the house, Catie stopped in the foyer and waited for Brenna to hang the coats before she asked, "What's going to happen to Uncle Cyrus?"

Brenna didn't have to hunch down as Ethan did when speaking with the girl for she was only a few inches taller. She lifted Catie's hand into her own and asked a question of her own. "What do you think should happen to him?"

Catie's shoulders tightened and then she shook her head. "I don't know. I don't think he's a good man. Uncle Cyrus came to see us a long time ago after he was in jail, but I haven't seen him since. Why is he looking for my pa?"

"That's something only your uncle and father can answer. It did sound as though your father and uncle saw each other more recently."

Catie's vehement shake of her head brought Brenna's arms around the girl. "It doesn't matter right now." She held the girl for a minute and then said, "I know what it's like to have a bad man in a family."

Catie pulled back a few inches, her light brown eyes misted

over. Brenna smoothed back a lock of hair from the young girl's brow. "My grandfather was not a good person, and he hurt a lot of people, people he was supposed to love and protect."

"Do you think because my Uncle Cyrus is bad, and maybe pa, too, that I might be bad?"

"We make our choices about what kind of person we will be in this life, and no one can take that choice from you, not even your family. You have a good heart and sharp mind, both of which I know you'll use wisely." Brenna used her handkerchief to wipe a tear from Catie's cheek. "Now, why don't we see if we can talk Amanda out of whatever smells so delicious."

Catie giggled and nodded before she wrapped her arms around Brenna's waist.

They talked Amanda out of two warm apple spice muffins, and then Amanda delighted Catie and Andrew each with a cup of hot chocolate while Brenna and Isabelle enjoyed a tea and conversation with Amanda. Catie studied Amanda. The soft brown hair tied neatly behind her neck reminded Catie of a picture she once saw of her own mother. Brenna's voice, like a sweet melody, made Catie long to hear her sing a lullaby. She heard one once while she waited for her father behind a train station. A woman on the platform sang to her baby, and it was the sweetest sound she had ever heard. Isabelle, and the way she looked at her younger brother, brought a rush of longing to have someone look at her with such love. Catie almost felt guilty wishing her ma had been more like one of these women. She glanced at each of them, her defenses strong, but weakening.

"Catie?"

She turned her head up at Brenna's soft voice.

"You wandered away for a few minutes." Brenna held out her hand. "I'd like to show you something."

Catie hesitated only a second before slipping her hand into Brenna's. They exited the kitchen and walked down the long hallway, turning into a large room. Catie had yet to see all of the house, but with a single glance at what lay before her, she knew this room would be her favorite. Eyes wide and mouth agape, Catie released Brenna's hand and stepped forward.

She'd never seen so many books in her life. She thought of the worn copy of *Little Women* next to the cot in her father's small cabin. The only gift he'd ever bought for her—after she promised never to ask for anything again—and it was likely gone now. Catie never did ask for anything else, and for five years that precious book had been her sole companion.

The magnificence before her rivaled anything she ever could have imagined. "Are these all yours?"

Brenna stepped up behind Catie, her presence a great comfort. "I suppose they don't belong to anyone. It's like everything else; we borrow it while we're on earth and then it goes to someone else."

Catie cautiously approached the first book-lined shelf and glanced over her shoulder. At Brenna's nod, Catie brushed her fingers over the spines. "How did you get so many?"

"I brought a few over from Scotland. Most of the books have been collected over many years and many generations. Do you know how to read, Catie?"

Catie turned and nodded. "I know a little."

Brenna moved to stand beside Catie and pulled a volume down from the shelf. *Black Beauty.*

"Who's Black Beauty?"

"He's a magnificent horse."

"What's it about?"

Brenna's beautiful smile lit up her green eyes. "That's for you to find out. It was one of my father's favorite books."

Catie held the book close to her chest. "Did he read it to you?"

"When this book was published, I was old enough to read it on my own, but he read other stories to me as a child. He especially liked telling me stories his parents and grandparents told him of faraway places, the old Highlanders who once roamed the Scottish hills—that's where I'm from—and he sometimes made up tales to amuse us. After my mother passed away, I spent many hours in our library. The books brought me comfort, and perhaps they will do the same for you."

Catie remained quiet and lifted the book out to admire it once again. "I promise to take good care of it." She looked up. "Will Uncle Cyrus come back?"

Brenna settled her arms around Catie, tentatively at first, but then embraced her. "I promise if you don't want to see him again, you won't have to."

Catie relaxed in Brenna's arms and closed her eyes. She didn't want to see her uncle again, but in her young heart, she believed her father would return. She had to believe because if she didn't, she'd have no one.

When Brenna left to find Ethan, Catie curled up in one of the large plaid chairs by the hearth surrounded the beautiful books. This is where Amanda found her when she came in and placed a plate of cookies and milk on the small table beside the chair.

"I reckon I should be working instead of reading."

"Nonsense. What you're doing is as important as any work." Amanda sat in the chair across from Catie and nodded toward the book. "What are you reading?"

"*Black Beauty.*"

"It's been ages since I've read that one."

Catie closed the book. "It's a little sad."

"It gets better." Amanda pointed to the cookies and milk. "Go ahead and enjoy a snack. If you're anxious to work, you can gather eggs for me in a short while. You already know where the hens are." Amanda's slow and teasing smile brought a faint blush to Catie's cheeks.

"I'd like to help." Catie took one of the cookies on the plate and bit into the molasses. "Where did you learn to cook?"

"Mostly from my mother, and I learned a few things on my own."

"How come you don't live with your family?" Catie's blush deepened the moment she asked. "My pa would have said it's not polite to ask."

Amanda smiled and leaned forward in the chair. "It's all right. My family is gone, but the Gallaghers are like my family now. You and I aren't so very different."

Catie's eyes narrowed with curiosity. "What do you mean?"

"I was searching for my own path when I arrived in Briarwood. One could say the Gallaghers found me and brought me home, like they did with you."

Catie finished the cookie and absently brushed crumbs away from her mouth. "But you got to stay."

Amanda nodded. "I chose to stay because I love them and this ranch. They gave me a home, work, and a family. Are you afraid you'll be sent away?"

Catie shrugged. "Maybe. I don't get to choose because I'm just a kid, right?"

"Children have more choices than they realize. If there's something you want more than anything in life, then you must do what you can to make it happen."

"And then it will come true?" Catie asked.

"Perhaps not right away, but someday it can be true if it's what you really want. You must have patience and believe in the people who want to help you." Amanda rose and smiled down at Catie. "Enjoy the cookies and then come and find me when you've read a few more chapters."

Catie watched Amanda leave the room before turning back to the book, but she could no longer concentrate on reading. If she wanted something more than anything, then she had to make it happen. She marked her place in the book and went to join Amanda.

Brenna found Ethan in the stable brushing down in his stallion. She knew from prior experience that he came out to spend time with his horse when something troubled him and he needed to work through the problem. If it was an issue related to ranch business, he immediately consulted with his brother or sister. When a personal issue arose, he preferred to spend time with his own counsel before sharing his thoughts with anyone else. Brenna knew that when Ethan was ready, he would share his troubles with her. However, on occasion she found he needed a little nudge.

The cold air brushed against Brenna's back as she stood in the doorway to the stable watching her husband. She knew the moment he realized he wasn't alone. He tossed the brush into a wooden bucket, smoothed his hand over the stallion's neck, and turned to her wearing a grin.

"You won't ever be able to sneak up on anyone when you smell like flowers in the winter." Ethan closed the distance between them and eased Brenna into his arms. He closed the door behind her, cutting off the cold breeze. He whispered against her hair, "I'm glad you're here, but it's freezing out here this morning." When he ran a hand through her hair, the sweet floral fragrance of her soap mingled with the scents of man and horse.

Brenna leaned up on her toes and pressed her lips to Ethan's. "The sun is peeking through and it's not terribly cold."

Ethan squeezed her gently and then stepped back. "You may

not mind the chill, but I imagine our unborn child might disagree."

Brenna silenced him with another kiss, this time lingering a few seconds longer. "Ye forget, me dear husband, that our bairn has Highland blood flowing through his veins. Those fierce storms put yer winters tae shame."

Ethan smiled at the heavy burr Brenna slipped into her soft accent. She peered around his larger frame and directed Ethan to another subject. "Why is the other horse saddled?"

"I'm going to meet up with Ben and Jake in town. Gabriel rode out to tell Ramsey and Eliza what's happened. I'd like to send a couple of wires and see that Ben has what he needs while at the jail. This gelding could use the exercise."

Brenna's small hand splayed gently over the side of Ethan's face. "You've not slept much these past few nights."

Ethan closed his eyes and turned into her hand, kissing her palm. "Between our ghost and Catie's family, I don't see an immediate end to the excitement."

"You don't really believe there's a ghost at Hawk's Peak, do you?"

Ethan laughed, a deep, rich sound she'd not heard in a few days. "Not a chance. You'll be careful on the ice?"

Brenna wrapped her arms around Ethan. "I won't endanger the baby. I was careless last week, but I promise I'm as surefooted on the ice as you are."

Ethan exhaled and nodded, though he seemed to have difficulty finding words. Brenna understood the emotions that coursed through Ethan every time they spoke of their unborn child because she experienced the same blend of excitement and trepidation. Neither of them feared having another child but rather that the peace they had found since Hunter—she long stopped thinking of him as her grandfather—had died wouldn't last. Brenna longed for this child to be born in a time without conflict, but as history has taught them, strife worked on no one's schedule but Fate's.

Hawk's Peak would be home to a new generation of Gallaghers and Camerons, and with tremendous hope came an undeniable worry. Eliza explained once to Brenna that no matter how large their herds or how plentiful their crops, they lived year in and year out at the mercy of the weather—a winter too harsh, a spring too heavy with rain, or a summer so dry that lightning sparks a flame. They could do nothing about the seasons except be prepared, and the Gallaghers made sure they were prepared for any contingency.

Brenna thoughts shifted to young Catie. Apprehension filled the young girl's eyes, but Brenna also saw within her a strength of will which rivaled any man born in America's rugged wilderness.

"Our children aren't the only ones who need looking after, Ethan."

"You're thinking of Catie." Ethan returned to his horse and led the animal into his stall. "She's been in my thoughts ever since I brought her home."

"What's going to happen with her uncle?"

Ethan closed the door on the stall and leaned against it. "He'll stay in jail for now."

"Without a sheriff?"

"Ben volunteered to take the first shift. We'll wire for the new marshal, but it could be days before he arrives. We'll wire the judge as well, but I'd like to keep him here awhile longer, at least until we know what he really wants."

"He wants Catie's father; he said as much."

Ethan walked to his wife and held her close when they left the stable. The wind had calmed to a gentle breeze, but the icy air still managed to cut through the outer layer of clothing. Ethan removed his coat and slipped it over Brenna's shoulders.

"The town is growing, and with talks of a spur line coming into Briarwood, it's probably time to consider hiring a sheriff."

"You don't sound happy about it."

"I know more tracks laid down in Montana means an easier time getting our cattle to market and working with buyers, but I'd just as soon keep the railroad out. I don't mind change, and I want what's best for our children's future, but I sometimes wonder if all this progress is best." Ethan smiled and held her close. "Don't mind me. I remember what this area was like when we first came to Hawk's Peak, and I don't want to see any of it change. This so-called progress makes it easier for men like Cyrus to come into town and stir up trouble."

Ethan kept his arm around Brenna as they walked in silence over broken ice and frozen mud toward the house.

Brenna intentionally slowed their pace. "What did you mean by what Cyrus really wants?"

"The kind of deep-rooted anger that drives a man to risk killing a young girl—his own kin—is about more than a little money owed. The men with Cyrus weren't farmers with pitchforks. They wore gunslinger rigs and knew how to shoot."

"Catie won't say she's scared, but I can see she is when she doesn't think I'm looking. Once upon a time I imagine she was a vivacious child, but now she bears her hardships as no child should."

Ethan rubbed his hands up and down Brenna's arms. "We'll find out what happened to her father."

"It's never a good time to lose a parent, but Christmas is especially difficult. I remember the first Christmas I spent without both my mother and father." Brenna leaned into her husband and took comfort in his loving embrace. What would have happened to her if the Gallaghers had not welcomed her into their lives when she first arrived in Briarwood? She couldn't imagine another life than the one she and Ethan had created together.

"I'd like for Catie to remain here until her father is found, and if he's not—" Brenna stepped back when Ethan pulled away, surprise evident in his eyes. "What is it?"

"Catie isn't going anywhere. If we find her father, we'll deal with him. As much as I'm pained to say this, if he left her alone once, I imagine he'd be open to another arrangement."

Brenna should have known Ethan wouldn't turn the girl away under any circumstances. "Will a judge allow Catie to remain here? She's terrified at the thought of going to an orphanage. I don't doubt she'd run away if given the chance."

"I'll speak with the judge and find out Catie's options." Ethan lifted Brenna's chin and lightly touched his lips to hers. "Let's not allow this to interfere with the holiday. Our family has much to be grateful for, especially this year. What about the Christmas celebration idea we talked about?"

Light and excitement touched Brenna's eyes. "With the town? So much has happened since then, I don't believe any of us gave it more consideration, but it's still a wonderful idea. It could help Catie to keep her mind and hands busy helping us."

Ethan's own smile eased into a thin line. "I agree, but as much as I want Catie to stay, we can't make the girl any promises until I've spoken with the judge."

"You promised her you'd find out what happened to her father," Brenna reminded him.

"I promise I'll do everything I can to ensure she never sees the inside of an orphanage."

8

Frost bestrewed the tranquil mountain town Ethan had called home since his parents brought them to the northern territory after the war. He'd witnessed a few changes over the years. Settlers arrived in Montana, hoping to make a new start, only to realize they weren't cut out for the cold north. They might last a season or two before they hightailed it back to from wherever they'd come. Railroad tracks would soon stretch across the breadth of Montana, making the land accessible to almost anyone, and eventually those who sought for statehood would get what they desperately wanted, but for now, Ethan was content with their quiet, little town.

Riffraff, from time to time, found their way to Briarwood, and even though there wasn't a full-time sheriff, they were dealt with quickly. Men like Nathan Hunter, who once had a stronghold in the area—and the money to hire as many men as he needed to do whatever bidding he wanted—weren't as easy to drive away. The Gallaghers didn't seek to control the land, but they would do whatever necessary to keep Briarwood and their home a safe place for the townsfolk and future generations.

Ethan caught up to the wagon a mile outside of town. His horse stomped at the frozen ground. Grooves from wagons were solidified in the earth by cold and ice, but the horses kept their footing. Ethan and Ben dismounted from their horses. Jake secured the wagon before moving around to the back bed where Cyrus had been tied up and made to sit next to his dead cohort. It rankled Ethan that one of the men managed to escape, and it was unlikely they'd find him in this weather.

"You coulda killed me! And, it ain't right making a man sit next to a dead body."

"Quiet, Cyrus." Ethan leaned against the side of the wagon. He hadn't planned to join Ben and Jake on the ride into town, but if Cyrus's rants about having other men willing—or stupid enough—to come looking for him, he wanted to be ready for them. "You're lucky a bullet didn't find you out there. It would have saved us a lot of trouble. Don't tempt me."

Ben managed to drag Cyrus from the wagon, while Ethan's finger rested near the trigger of his rifle. Jake told Ethan he was going to take the body over to Doc Brody's, and he'd return soon. Everyone ignored Cyrus as Ben dragged him onto the boardwalk.

"You ain't got no right! You ain't the law."

Ethan followed the small group into the jailhouse. "Unfortunately for you, we're what passes for the law in these parts." Ethan waited until Cyrus was locked up in a cell before lowering his gun. "Now, what does a worthless child killer like you want with Catie's father?"

"I ain't no child killer!"

Ethan's eyes narrowed and he stepped closer to the bars. "Had I not been there, you or one of your men might have shot the girl."

"She's my kin. You ain't got no say in matters between kin."

"It's your unlucky day, Cyrus, because it so happens we've taken an interest in seeing the girl is kept safe." Ethan leaned back against the wall, one leg relaxed, and his hand resting on his holster. "What do you want with her father?"

"Don't matter to you or anybody else. He's my brother."

"Regardless, you've made this our business when you rode onto our land. It was well within our right to shoot you dead, so I'll ask you again, what do you want with Catie and her father?"

Cyrus lunged at the bars and shook, but his pathetic effort did little more than shake dust from the ceiling.

"You see, Cyrus, one of the men who rode in with us is over at the telegraph office wiring the sheriff in Bozeman. It seems there's a Railway Circular out on you."

Ethan watched Cyrus pale. "You shouldn't have ridden onto our land, Cyrus."

"Suppose I have information that would be valuable to a lawman."

"You could have killed your niece. I don't need any other information."

"I know who robbed that train down Butte way last month. They ain't never caught the men."

Ethan, bored now with Cyrus, shook his head. "You could name any bandit wanted by the law. Without proof, your word doesn't mean a thing."

"It was Joseph Carr. I swear on the gold he stole from me that he done it."

"You'd accuse your own brother?"

"I swear he done it."

Ethan considered the man. "The word of a killer isn't worth the breath you used to speak it."

Ben stepped into the small back room where one of the two cells was now occupied by Cyrus. "We got a reply from the sheriff in Bozeman. He's sending two deputies, but it seems Cyrus here is also wanted by the U.S. Marshals. A marshal was killed on the train he and his gang robbed."

Ethan turned back to Cyrus. "How about that. Your time is up, Cyrus." Ethan started to follow Ben into the office, but Cyrus hadn't said his last word.

"I'll kill you, Gallagher."

Ethan turned slowly, his movements those of a bored man, but his deep blue eyes revealing another story.

"I heard about you Gallaghers. You think you're better than everyone, but you ain't."

"Not better than everyone, Cyrus, just the likes of you." Ethan moved closer to the cell and lowered his voice to a whisper. His drawn pistol rested against his side, pointed at the prisoner. "If you heard about us, it was from others like you, which means you know what happens to men who try to hurt our family."

Cyrus lowered his gaze to the pistol and then raised his eyes back up to meet Ethan's.

"Do we understand each other?"

Cyrus stepped away from the bars and nodded. "I'm still goin' to kill him."

"Your brother won't die by your hands, at least while you're in here." Ethan joined Ben and Jake in the outer office, and secured the door between them and the cells. Someone had started a fire in the small stove, and warmth began to thaw the winter air that had crept into the building. He looked to Ben. "Did the sheriff say how long it would take his deputies to arrive?"

"There's a storm down in Bozeman that will slow them down some."

Ethan nodded. "Then we've got a long night ahead of us. I'd like two of us at a time in case any more of Cyrus's friends—if he has any—decide to show up."

A brief glance passed between Ben and Jake before Ben said, "We'll stay here with him, Ethan. You should be home with your family."

Ethan shook his head. "We should all be home instead of here. Except, if it happens on Gallagher land, a Gallagher is responsible."

"We know how it works, but with your wife in her condition and now the little girl under your care, we figure you can make an exception this time."

Ethan sat on the edge of the desk and considered his foreman. Ben Stuart had been the foreman at Hawk's Peak long enough to have earned the right to speak his mind. Ben wasn't wrong; Ethan worried about Brenna every time she tried to overdo around the house or walked outside alone on the ice. This would be their second child, so Brenna obviously knew to be careful. Except, he would never forget the sight of his wife and unborn child falling on the ice after the first snowfall. He knew his incessant worrying made Brenna daft, but Ethan couldn't stop from exerting his concern as both a husband and father.

"All right, Ben," Ethan said with some reservation. "You've been deputized in the past, so you'll remain in charge. Ramsey is the only one with any type of legal authority, so I'll let him know what's happened when I return to the ranch." Ethan looked around the large room from the study desk on which he sat to wanted posters tacked to the wall. "Never thought I'd say this, but it's time we found a sheriff, someone more permanent." Ethan pushed away from the desk and stood. "I'll be sure you're relieved tomorrow."

"Don't worry about a thing, Ethan."

Ethan nodded, despite knowing he would worry until Cyrus became someone else's problem. They needed to learn more about Catie's past and locate her father. No matter how much he wanted to believe her, he sensed the girl was holding back, though not on purpose.

Ethan left the relative comfort of the jailhouse for the frozen streets of Briarwood. The sun hovered low over the mountains, and Ethan estimated he had about an hour before it was too dark and dangerous to ride home. Most folks had found their way home or into the saloon for a drink or the café for a hot meal.

The boardwalk rattled slightly under Ethan's hurried footsteps. A bell above the door of the telegraph office jingled as he stepped through.

"Hello, Mr. Gallagher."

Ethan smiled at the young man behind the telegraph counter. "Hello, Foster. Is your father around?"

"He took Ma to a nice meal over at the hotel for their anniversary. I was just about to close up. Is there something I can do for you?"

Ethan reached for the small pad of paper and pencil Orin Lloyd, their new telegraph operator since his cousin decided to retire, kept convenient for patrons. "I'll write out what I need, and you can give it to your father."

Foster leaned over the counter to glimpse the paper. "I can send the telegram for you. Pa taught me real good, and I'm his official apprentice. I sent three just today."

Ethan grinned at the young man. "You plan to take over for him one day?"

Foster nodded. "I sure do. Pa says a man has to have a skill, and folks are always going to communicate."

"He's correct." Ethan passed the written message to Foster. "This is going to Judge Welby in Bozeman."

Foster read over Ethan's words and looked up. "You found a girl?"

Ethan nodded and studied the young man. "She's about your age, Foster. I don't suppose you've heard of a family around here, down on their luck with a daughter called Catie."

"I sure haven't, but there's a lots of folks down on their luck right now. Pa said more and more are coming into these parts thinking to farm and ranch. He calls them greenhorns."

Ethan chuckled. "Will you check with your father as well? He gets a lot of the news before the rest of us."

"He sure does, Mr. Gallagher." Foster held up the paper. "I'll send this straightaway, and I won't tell anybody. Pa taught me about a telegraph operator's oath of silence, to keep things private and such."

"I appreciate that. You have a good evening, Foster." At the door, his hand on the knob, Ethan turned. "What does your family do for Christmas?"

Caught off guard by the question, Foster set the pad of paper down and stared at Ethan. "Well, sir, we do what other folks do I guess. My pa and I cut down a tree a few days before Christmas Eve. We hunt up something special. Ma makes pies and plays the piano so we can sing."

"Sounds like a fine way to spend Christmas."

Foster nodded slowly. "It's my favorite time of year."

"Mine, too." Ethan said his final goodbye and left the telegraph office. Up and down the main street through town, Ethan saw candles burning in some of the windows, ribbons and greenery hanging from porches and over doorways. With rooftops coated in a light layer of snow, Briarwood was the image of one of those holiday cards Loren carried in his general store.

He remembered a time in his youth, long before his parents passed, when the town put up a big tree in the meadow near the church. Ethan couldn't recall the last Christmas the town had put up a tree, except that it was before his parents died. Had it been his parents' doing during those years? he wondered. Christmas at Hawk's Peak had become a grand tradition for him and his family, and Ethan was embarrassed to admit he didn't know what most of the townspeople did on this special holiday. Granted, they'd had a lot of distractions over the years, but the Gallagher family had always been seen as patrons of the town. If there was ever a time of year to do more, it was Christmas.

The women's plan of hosting a Christmas party for the town was fast becoming the best idea they'd had in a long time. They had much to be thankful for this year: Nathan Hunter was gone, Elizabeth was free to live her life reunited with her grandchildren, Eliza and Ramsey now enjoyed wedded bliss, Gabriel and Isabelle would soon be in their own house, and Ethan thought with a broad smile on his lips, another generation of Gallaghers would assure the family's legacy continued.

Ethan returned to the jail for his horse, mounted, and with one last look around the quiet town, he raised the collar of his shearling to block the wind from his neck and headed toward home.

9

Ethan sauntered into his brother's home, or what would be his home in another week. He'd made a habit of stopping by for a short time each night at the new place to check on the progress. Gabriel was determined to finish the home so Isabelle and Andrew could wake up in the new year in a home they'd built together. Even though they'd spend every holiday together, and had been apart before, it wasn't the same as waking up under one roof.

Ethan looked around at the new furniture—some built by Gabriel, other pieces ordered from San Francisco or Boston. The house would remain sparse until the remainder of the furnishings arrived. However, it already felt like a real home.

Gabriel looked up when Ethan walked into the room. "I expected you to be home by now. Ramsey's there now with Eliza. Elizabeth's fattening everyone up, though she excused me to work on the house. Lucky me."

Ethan laughed. "Elizabeth is enjoying a house full of family these days, and she's definitely making up for lost time. Speaking of the house, it looks good—great in fact. You've really been putting in a lot extra hours." Ethan ran his hand over one of the papered walls in Isabelle's new parlor.

"So have you. Didn't think I wouldn't notice that the kitchen was completed, or the last bedroom upstairs was papered?"

Ethan shrugged. "Ramsey and I had a little time. Besides, I still feel guilty that I'm the one staying in the main house."

"Don't be." Gabriel gave his brother a friendly squeeze of the shoulder. "Eliza and I knew the house was yours—it was meant to be—and I wanted to do this for Isabelle and Andrew. They had to leave so much behind after their parents passed; I want them to wake up each day knowing this is a place they'll never have to leave and that no one can take away from them."

"It's a fine home, Gabe. You should be proud." Ethan leaned over the plans his brother had spread out over a makeshift table—furniture sketches. "You're still building furniture? I thought you'd finished the last piece that wasn't . . . wait a minute, a cradle?" He stood straight and stared at his brother. "Is Isabelle—"

"Pregnant?" Gabriel grinned. "You aren't supposed to know yet."

"Well, congratulations." Ethan pulled his brother into a hug and slapped him a couple of times on the back. "My little brother, all grown up."

"You better keep it to yourself. Isabelle has a plan worked out to tell everyone, and she says the moment isn't quite right."

"Promise you won't wait too long. I don't know how long I can keep this kind of secret."

"You can."

"Not from Brenna."

Gabriel rolled up the house plans and tucked them into a desk drawer. "It won't be too long. Isabelle's waiting to announce the news at Christmas."

"I don't think I can keep this from Brenna for two more weeks. How about—"

"I mean it, Ethan. Isabelle swore me to secrecy. Obviously I failed, but I'm swearing you to it. She'll have my hide if she finds out I told you first."

"Technically you didn't tell me, I figured it out." At Gabriel's glower, Ethan held up his hands and laughed. "Don't worry, I promise. I'd better get back to the house and let everyone know what's going on in town."

Gabriel rolled up the furniture sketch and added it to a stack of papers. "I'll head back with you. I promised Isabelle I wouldn't take too long over here tonight. She hasn't been feeling too well the past couple of days."

"Neither has Brenna." Ethan and his brother stepped outside, and with Ethan's stallion walking alongside them, they made their way over the snowy pasture to the main house. Pine-scented air filled Ethan's lungs. The stars overhead twinkled in the black sky, but he predicted those stars would soon be hidden behind snow clouds. The stream flowed freely, cracking bits of ice along its edges. "You picked a great spot, Gabe."

"I didn't, not exactly. I gave Andrew three choices, and this is the one he picked."

"You let Andrew choose?"

Gabriel nodded and stuffed his hands into the pockets of his coat. "Isabelle and I made the first three choices, so it was only fair to let Andrew help, too. I didn't know the kid's eyes could get so big."

"It won't be long before he's mending fences and breaking horses. He's such a great kid."

"Isabelle will have our hides if we rush his growing up." Gabriel's words said one thing, but his smile said he liked having a woman to fuss and worry over him and the boy. "He spends more time with his new pup than he does with the horses, but Isabelle thinks it's only a matter of time before Andrew is wrangling cattle with his dog running beside him. She wants Andrew to attend university, so help me out a little when Andrew decides he wants to spend more time with the cattle than with his studies."

Ethan shrugged. "It didn't hurt us any."

Gabriel's laughter filled the night air. "I seem to recall a fiery argument you had with Father about leaving the ranch. For a while there I thought you might defy him."

"I considered it, for about five seconds. Most of that was me blustering." They walked into the stable where Ethan removed the saddle and bridle from his stallion. Once the horse was brushed, fed, and secure in his stall, they locked up the stable for the night.

"You've changed, though, Ethan. Time was you'd be less bluster and more bite."

Ethan stopped and faced his brother. His recent joviality had been replaced by a seriousness Ethan suspected would deepen within him for years to come. "Time was, I didn't care about anything other than my family and this ranch. The rest of the world . . . I gave it little thought. Life changes—Brenna changed mine, and then Jacob. Despite the anguish and the loss, those changes have been good as our outlook on life takes another path."

"Do you ever think about what might have been, had they not died so young?"

Ethan thought about their father who survived a war and their mother who kept the family together during those devastating years. "Sometimes. I remember their last Christmas with us, except no one realized it would be our last one together."

"I remember the tree Eliza picked out that year. It wouldn't fit in the house." He sobered. "It was also one of the coldest winters we'd had in three years."

Ethan nodded. "We went out with Father on Christmas Eve to search for that missing family who tried to leave town before the storm hit."

"We found them, too."

"Half dead," Ethan murmured. "They were huddled together so tight I didn't think we'd be able to pull them apart."

"When we returned home, all we wanted to do was sleep."

Ethan's smile spread slowly. "But Father wouldn't let Mother down, and she didn't want us to keel over during supper. They wanted to make each other happy." Ethan looked toward the stars once more and in a moment of sentimentality, he wondered if any of them were his parents. "I didn't understand it—not really—until I met Brenna." He turned back to his brother. "You always understood, though."

Gabriel shrugged. "I didn't have your burdens." He slapped a hand on Ethan's shoulder, his straight, white teeth shown through a lopsided grin. "We should have these talks more often."

Ethan swiped his brother's hand away but did so with a smile. "Not if you know what's good for you." He started walking again toward the house. "Thanks."

"Anytime."

They continued forward, Ethan's gaze shifting to the bunkhouse. Every window across the way was lit up. "Poker night?"

Gabriel nodded. "Guess it is. Been a while since I missed one." But instead of heading for the bunkhouse, Gabriel followed Ethan up the porch steps and into the house. It wasn't too long ago when the brothers would have played poker with the boys well into the night, but Ethan suspected these days Gabriel would rather spend those cold winter nights with Isabelle. Ethan knew the feeling all too well.

Brenna turned toward Ethan when he slipped beneath the covers, and he welcomed her into his embrace.

"You've been gone awhile."

Ethan pressed a kiss to the top of her head and pulled her closer. "The ride back took a bit longer than I planned. Snow's coming."

He could feel her lips curve into a smile against his chest. "Snow is always coming this time of year. Did you say goodnight to Jacob?"

Ethan's body relaxed and he closed his eyes. "I swear he got bigger today."

Brenna's lyrical laughter brought a smile to his own lips. "It does seem that way. I predict he'll be as tall as his pa one day."

Ethan grinned at the idea. "I had hoped to speak with Catie when we arrived home, but no one was downstairs."

"I imagine Ramsey and Eliza are still awake, but the rest of us were close to falling asleep at the kitchen table after dinner." Brenna raised her head to look at her husband. "Elizabeth left you a plate covered near the oven."

"I found it."

"Is everything all right?"

Ethan stared into his wife's deep green eyes. "It's been a difficult year for some of the families in Briarwood."

"It's a hard life here. You know that better than anyone." Brenna laid her arm over her husband's chest and rested her chin on top. "When I first arrived, I remember thinking how both alike and dissimilar Montana was to Scotland."

Ethan's fingers moved through Brenna's long, auburn hair, and trailed down her back. He remembered her arrival with great fondness, and though it took nearly losing her to realize his life meant little without her in it, Ethan also remembered the adjustments she had to make. He had spent a few months in Scotland awaiting the birth of their son, and he, too, had marveled at the similarities, even as he respected what Brenna gave up to live with him in Montana.

Brenna continued, "Had it not been for you and your family,

I doubt I could have made a life here. Parts of this land have been built up into small cities, but for many, Montana is still rugged and untamed territory."

"Do you ever regret leaving Scotland?"

"Not for a moment."

Her immediate answer eased him, but she wasn't finished speaking.

"I do miss Scotland, but I wouldn't live my life apart from you for anything or any place. We know my situation is a unique one. I was blessed with wealth, and I took that for granted until I came here. There are women like Amanda who travel here alone with no money, no prospects, and somehow fight their way through and survive. Then there are widows, like Mrs. Johnson whose husband died last week in a hunting accident. She has no children and no other kin. People will help where they can, but winter will be hard for her."

Ethan leaned up. "I had heard Mrs. Johnson was going to live with her sister's family in Oregon."

"When we were in town a few days ago so that Grandmother could visit with Mrs. Johnson, she told us that her sister's husband worried there wouldn't be enough room. They promised to send her a little money instead so she could remain in her house."

"Why didn't Elizabeth say anything?"

Brenna smiled softly and pressed a light kiss to Ethan's lips. "Because she knows you well enough now to know you'd not only give Mrs. Johnson money, but do your best to find her another husband or set her up with enough funds to live a comfortable life if she preferred not to remarry."

"I'm not that predictable."

"I love that you are so predictable, at least when it comes to helping others. It's a fine attribute. Grandmother realizes that we can't take in everyone who needs a home or give money to everyone without, even though your big heart wants to do just that."

Ethan gazed fondly at his wife and then narrowed his eyes. "You gave Mrs. Johnson money."

Brenna's fair cheeks brightened to an attractive shade of rose red. "Not exactly. I gave money to Reverend Philips who will see that she's looked after through winter and won't have to leave her home, at least until a better situation can be discovered in spring. I didn't want to embarrass her or for her to feel obligated to repay. I know we're supposed to make money decisions together, but—"

Ethan pressed a finger to his wife's lips. "But nothing. Even with the new horse breeding expansion and Gabriel's new house, this family has more than we could possibly need or spend on our own—more than our children will need for their futures. I can't think of a better use for the money your parents' left you than to help others." Ethan settled back against the pillow and slid his arm around Brenna's shoulders. "There's another under our roof who I'd like to help, but I doubt it's going to be as easy a solution as bolstering the church coffers."

"How long will it take to hear back from the judge?"

"I don't know. A part of me hopes the whole matter is delayed until after Christmas. It would be nice to see her enjoy the holiday, especially since everything afterward is uncertain."

"Will you look for her father?"

Ethan nodded. "Ramsey still has contact with the marshal's office. I'm hoping that if he reached out to them directly, it will be more official than if a citizen reaches out. I don't want to cause problems for Catie's father just because he's Cyrus's brother. He may be innocent of the crimes for which Cyrus has accused him."

"I worry for her. She wants to engage, but it's seems as though she expects, and is waiting, for bad news."

"When you've spent most of your young life on the receiving

end of sorrow, I imagine waiting for it comes as second nature."

Brenna released a slow breath and closed her eyes. "How blessed our Jacob is for his family. If anything ever happened to either us, there is no shortage of family willing to love and raise him. I wonder . . . do you hear that?"

Ethan listened but heard nothing. "I suspected a storm and the wind—"

"It's not the wind. The singing." Brenna threw back the covers and nearly tripped over the lace hem of her nightgown in her haste to leave the bed.

"Brenna, wait!" Ethan hurried to put on the pants he discarded earlier and followed his wife from the bedroom. He glimpsed the white of her nightgown before she slipped into the nursery. Ethan's steps faltered when he entered Jacob's room. Brenna peered over his crib, but it was the slight movement of the rocking chair beside the crib that drew Ethan's notice. "Is he all right?"

Brenna nodded as Ethan walked up to stand beside her. Together they gazed upon their sleeping son. "It was just the wind." But when Ethan checked the windows, each one was securely fastened.

"I know the difference between a woman singing and the wind." Brenna remained by her son's bed, unwilling to leave him alone.

Ethan's romantic plans for the evening would have to be put on hold. "We can bring Jacob's crib into our room for the night."

"You'd need to wake Ramsey or Gabriel for that." Brenna held onto her husband's arms when he wrapped them around her waist. "He's peaceful. Whatever it was I heard didn't bother him in the least."

"If you ask me, he's smiling."

Brenna studied the gentle rise and fall of her son's chest, and the slight upturn of his small, red lips. "So he is. We've done well, my love."

Ethan turned her into his arms. "We have, and I'll give most of that credit to you. Let's hope we can do just as well for Catie."

"Speaking of Catie, I have an idea—"

A crash echoed through the house. Brenna glanced down at her son to be sure he still slept. "Please tell me you heard that."

Ethan nodded. "I heard it. Stay here with Jacob."

Brenna might have argued had it not been for their son, but she agreed and stood in front of the crib like a soldier guarding their last defense. Ethan rushed to his room first for a shirt. Back in the hallway, he ran into Ramsey who stayed the night. "Where's Eliza."

"Still asleep."

"Good. Gabriel sleeps like the dead, and I'd rather not wake anyone else until we know what happened."

Ramsey agreed. "It could be that something just fell over."

"We'll see." Ethan headed down the stairs first, not as certain as Ramsey that nothing was amiss. Then again, there were enough people living under one roof that it wasn't inconceivable someone was awake and had an accident. Immediately thinking of Catie wandering in an unfamiliar house, he hurried down the last few steps. Silence and shadows met them at the base of the stairs. Fires burning low in the kitchen and main living room of the house helped to dispel the darkness.

Ramsey walked down the hall toward the kitchen while Ethan made his way down the opposite hall to the front of the house. The fire in the front room continued to burn, stronger than it should have. "Anyone here?"

A shadow by one of the large stuffed chairs faced the hearth. A dainty head peeked around the side of a chair, sleek blond hair falling to one side. "Ethan? I'm sorry, did I wake you?"

Ethan expelled a slow and steady breath. "Isabelle. No . . . did you hear a loud crash a few minutes ago?"

Isabelle rose, but she looked as though she might not be able to stand on her own. Ethan rushed forward to help. "Thank you. I wasn't feeling quite right, so I came downstairs for tea. I didn't want to wake Gabriel and worry him."

"Is everything all right with . . ." He almost let her secret slip.

Isabelle smiled, and though her eyes sparkled, Ethan could see the weariness beneath. "Gabriel told you."

"Not intentionally." Ethan released his sister-in-law. "Are you all right?"

"Oh, I'm fine. It's part of the experience, or so Brenna tells me." Isabelle looked to the doorway when Ramsey walked into the room. "What did you mean about a crash?"

Ramsey came in and said, "I didn't see anything."

Ethan explained to Isabelle, "It sounded like something falling over, but it could have been outside. The wind has picked up. You didn't hear anything down here?"

Isabelle shook her head. "Not a thing. I'd best get back upstairs and try to get some sleep."

Ethan nodded absently but stopped her at the door. It seemed that his concern for pregnant women extended to his sister-in-law, an affliction that was likely to extend to all the women in the family. If there was anything to worry about, it would be downstairs and not up. "Would you please let Brenna know I'll be up soon and she can go back to bed?"

Isabelle gave him a curious look but didn't ask for further explanation. "Of course."

When she left the room, Ethan said to Ramsey, "I'm going to take a look outside."

"I'll go with you. In this snow, it'll go faster with two. If we find nothing, let's not worry about it tonight."

They pulled on their boots and outer clothing before stepping into the first swirling flakes of a snowstorm. They walked in opposite directions, but when Ethan reached the point where they would have met up, Ramsey was nowhere to be seen.

10

"**B**oss?"

Ethan glanced over his shoulder, the familiar face not who he expected. "Colton?"

"I was coming in from checking on the stable when I saw the lantern. Glad to see it's you."

"Ramsey's around here somewhere. Did you hear anything else tonight?"

Colton shook his head and looked up at the sky, heavy with thick flakes. He raised his voice to carry above the noise. "Not likely to with this wind, except maybe a gunshot, and I didn't hear one of those."

"Is anyone else awake?"

"A few of the boys who don't have the first shift tomorrow." Colton trudged through the snow to stand directly in front of Ethan. "Where'd you say Ramsey was?"

"Taking too long to get here. Ramsey!" Ethan's futile shout came back to him over the wind. Together, he and Colton covered the distance as quickly as the snow allowed. Colton nearly tripped over something compressed in the snow.

"Damn." Ethan knelt down over Ramsey's prone body. "Send up three shots and then try to get him out of the snow and inside. I need to get back!"

Ethan relived his worst nightmare in the few minutes it took him to get to the back door that led into the kitchen. It wasn't so long ago when Tyre Burton, one of Nathan Hunter's men who turned on him, had managed to capture Eliza and hold her inside the ranch. Ethan swore his family wouldn't have to relive a similar nightmare.

Inside, Gabriel almost tripped down the stairs, half-awake and half-dressed.

"What's going on? I heard the shots. Eliza's upstairs with Brenna and Jacob."

"Isabelle?"

"Fell asleep as soon as she crawled into bed."

"Ramsey and I both heard something. So did Brenna. We went outside to investigate. Ramsey ended up with a gash on his head, unconscious in the snow. Colton's with him now."

Ethan looked around the quiet halls and heard nothing but creaks and the faint sound of the wind through the windows. "No one's in here."

The look Gabriel cast Ethan was justified in Ethan's opinion. If Gabriel had told him the same story, he might think his brother was hearing things.

"Gabe, will you humor me and look around upstairs and down here once more to make sure the house is secure? I'm going to help Colton with Ramsey."

Eliza dabbed whiskey onto a clean cloth and placed the bottle on the kitchen table. She gave her brother a look Ethan only saw when she was especially annoyed with him. He knew her well, though, and recognized the annoyance only served to mask her worry. Anger would come once she finished tending to Ramsey.

"You should have woken us."

Ramsey flinched only slightly when Eliza pressed the cloth

against the gash on the back of her husband's head.

"Did you see who it was?" Gabriel asked.

Ramsey started to shake his head, but then held still for Eliza's ministrations. "I heard someone behind me, but before I could see his face, everything went black. He was a big man, closer to your height, Ethan."

Ethan listened to Brenna's voice as it carried downstairs. It was young Jacob's favorite lullaby. Most of the household had awakened when Colton sent the three gunshots into the air, and the rest woke when Jacob squalled for attention. Elizabeth refused to go back to sleep, but she compromised by checking on her great-grandson. Ethan thought it best not to worry her about Ramsey's injury until Eliza finished tending the wound. Amanda offered to prepare coffee, assuring them she wouldn't be able to sleep until everyone else retired. Colton had roused the other men to search the out buildings, their task made easier when the heavy snowfall subsided to light flurries. The clock rang half past midnight.

"You need a few stitches, Ramsey." Eliza glanced over her shoulder at Ethan. "I need thread and needle; Brenna keeps hers in the parlor."

Amanda said, "Mine is here." She went to the far corner of the kitchen and lifted a small basket onto the table. She withdrew her smallest needle and finest thread. She poured some of the whiskey over the needle, threaded the small eye, and set the needle on a clean cloth spread over the table. She then placed a bowl of hot water next to more fresh cloths.

Eliza glanced up at her. "You'd make a fine nurse."

"My mother was a nurse in the war."

Ethan walked into the kitchen in time to hear Amanda's confession. She rarely talked about her life before arriving in Briarwood, and they never pressed her. He'd watched the growing affection between Amanda and Ben, but his foreman had not yet been successful in breaking through Amanda's mysterious past.

Eliza rose from her chair and stepped closer to Ramsey, threaded needle in hand. "You'll want to take that drink now."

Instead, Ramsey rested his hands on his knees and sat completely still. "Go ahead, love, I won't move."

True to his word, Ramsey didn't move while Eliza sewed seven stitches just below his hairline. Once finished, she accepted a clean cloth dipped in hot water from Amanda and cleaned around the wound. She then pressed a cloth directly below the wound and slowly poured whiskey over the stitches. This time, Ramsey visibly winced and swore under his breath.

"You'll thank me later." Eliza put aside the whiskey and lowered herself to the chair. "We need to wrap that in a minute."

Ramsey shook his head.

Eliza smiled sweetly. "It wasn't a suggestion."

Ethan smiled at the interchange between the two of them. "I'm going out to help with the search."

"I'll go with you. I just want to look in on Isabelle."

Eliza watched Gabriel leave the room and then turned and looked up at Ethan. "If they haven't found anything yet, chances are any trace of whoever did this is covered with snow."

"You'd rather we didn't look."

"Oh, you should look, but leave the slimy—"

"Eliza."

Ethan nodded toward Amanda, and Eliza's color rose.

"Sorry, Amanda."

"I've heard worse." Amanda began to tidy up. "I'll go and look in on Elizabeth and Catie."

Ethan walked over to the stove where Amanda had brewed a fresh pot of coffee. He filled two cups and set them both on the table. To Ramsey he said, "You'll want to stay up awhile. I've seen men with head injuries get sick and dizzy afterward. It isn't pretty."

Back outside with his men, Ethan received a full—and disappointing—report from Colton.

"The men didn't find anything. There were a few tracks—Ramsey was right about it being a tall man—where we found Ramsey in the snow. I was able to follow them to the lean-to by the wood shack, and then whoever it was rode out on a horse."

"The bastard certainly knew what he was doing."

Colton nodded. "He didn't leave much of a trail. I could tell that he started to ride northeast. The snow will have covered most of his tracks by now, but there are others signs I can follow to get a fix on where he went."

Neither moon nor stars could break through the thick blanket of clouds above them. Colton was their best tracker and hunter, yet even he couldn't find invisible tracks on a night like this. "It's too dark and too dangerous, Colton. We'll head out at first light."

Colton hesitated before saying, "I've tracked in worse conditions. If this man circles back around, he could do worse than strike Ramsey over the head."

Why knock out one man and then leave? Ethan wondered. It served no other purpose than to put the ranch on alert. Even the drifters would know a spread the size of Hawk's Peak would have enough men to cause problems for any rustler or thief. Only one thing at the ranch had changed in the past few days—Catie. First Cyrus, and now this stranger. Perhaps it was the third rider who managed to escape.

Ethan rubbed his eyes against the sting of exhaustion. "We'll wait for the light and then you and I will ride out with one of the men."

Brenna managed to drift to sleep, but Ethan only managed a brief nap before he woke again, several hours before the sun would make an appearance.

He padded down the stairs, fully clothed, and slipped into the kitchen where Elizabeth sat with a cup of something hot steaming from one of the fancy teacups she favored. "I didn't expect anyone else to be up."

Elizabeth lowered the cup and saucer on the table and rose. "I've made some coffee."

"I'll take it." Ethan watched Elizabeth with wary eyes while she moved with ease around the kitchen. She handed him a filled mug, steam rising from the top. "Is everything all right, Elizabeth?"

"I'd like to know, myself. I saw a stack of kitchen cloths soaking in the sink. Looked like blood."

Ethan lowered himself into the chair beside Elizabeth. "We didn't want to worry you."

Elizabeth looked him over. "It doesn't appear to have been you. Who was injured?"

"Ramsey. Don't worry, he's fine. Just a bump on the head that looked worse than it was."

"Someone should have told me," Elizabeth said in a tone reserved for grandmothers.

Ethan nodded and released a quick breath. "It was my call, and I'm sorry for it. I figured you've been through more than enough already. I promise, it won't happen again."

"Good. And for the record, I'm grateful that you want to shield me. My Brenna is lucky to have you." Elizabeth patted his cheek, rose once more, and said, "You'll have some breakfast before you go off and do whatever foolish thing you have planned."

Ethan grinned and drank his coffee, deciding it was better not to argue with her.

Half an hour later, with a stomach full of eggs, ham, and

Elizabeth's sourdough biscuits, Ethan ventured outside. The wind had subsided, and the snow clouds cleared away to reveal a starry sky. The storm had left them with a blanket of fresh snow. It was rare these days when Ethan felt as though he was the only one on the ranch. Except for the occasional low from the cattle, silence settled over the earth. Ethan closed his eyes and inhaled deeply, the cold air a welcome shock to his lungs. He loved the way the ranch smelled in the winter; always like Christmas with the mingling of pine, snow, and the slow burn of morning fires from the chimneys. He leaned against one of the thick log posts holding up the front porch roof and gazed over the moonlit land. The years of memories since his parents' passing rushed back to him.

Time stood still at Hawk's Peak despite people who would try to change it, claiming progress was best for the future of Montana Territory. Of course, they'd modernized when necessary to keep the ranch producing and competing with other ranches, but Ethan was content to keep most of the modern world at bay.

The last argument Ethan had with his father was about him attending university in the East. He wanted to remain at the ranch, but his father wouldn't relent. Jacob Gallagher, his son's namesake, had been right on most occasions when it came to the best interests of his children. Now that Ethan had a son of his own, he understood a father's desire to give his children every opportunity to be successful in life. An education helped Ethan to make wise decisions regarding the ranch, and it would do the same for his son.

What would his father think of Hawk's Peak now? Ethan smiled at the idea, and with a lantern in hand, stepped down from the porch to begin his day. Smoke rose from the chimney of the large bunkhouse and a single set of footprints marred the fresh snow. Ethan pulled opened the stable door and stepped inside to where a dim light shone.

"And here I thought I was the only one fool enough to be out here this early."

Colton grinned. "Couldn't sleep. Something about the tracks has been bothering me."

"What do you mean?"

Colton rested an arm over his saddled horse. "On the way back from the bunkhouse, I took one more look around and found more prints beneath some of the windows on the first level, like someone had been waiting. Glass from a broken bottle was beneath the window—possibly what you heard. When I was with Ramsey, there were other prints in the snow, like the man had knelt down. My guess is that Ramsey surprised whoever hit him, and it appears they checked to make sure they didn't hurt him too badly."

Ethan had learned to trust Colton's instincts when it came to tracking and understanding of the person behind those tracks. Raised first by an old widow who taught him to read and write, and then taken in by a trapper and miner who rarely left the mountains, Colton could track a single bear across the breadth of the territory before he was fifteen. A lot of years in between— a time Colton didn't talk about—had done nothing to diminish his abilities. Ethan had relied on those skills numerous times, especially when there was imminent danger. Ethan was confident with Colton's assessment of their mysterious visitor.

"You think you can track him?"

Colton nodded without hesitation. "Snow covered the tracks, but evidence that a horse and rider traveled through the pastures will still be noticeable."

The stable door slid open, a slice of frigid air swept inside. "Didn't think you'd have fun without me, did you?" Gabriel wore a wide grin as he sauntered toward his brother and Colton. "Elizabeth woke the household with her cooking. Hope you said good morning to your wife before you slipped out."

"I did. How's Isabelle feeling?"

"Better. She's talked Catie into sitting in on a lesson with Andrew after breakfast." Gabriel rubbed his gloved hands together. "Speaking of Catie, something's gnawing at her. She was helping Brenna with Jacob when I left."

Ethan looked from his brother to his stallion and back. "Will you saddle him up for me and meet me out front? I just need a few minutes."

"Sure thing."

Ethan waded back through the fresh snow, stepping in the prints he'd already made to the stable. Where a short while ago, the house had been quiet, it now bustled with activity. The fires had been stoked in every hearth, women's voices filled the halls, and the most delectable fragrance wafted from the back of the house. Ethan made a beeline to the kitchen, the center of the activity.

Everyone save Brenna, Catie, and Jacob sat around the long wooden table in various stages of their morning meal.

"You're a sight," Eliza said over her half-empty plate. "Problem?"

Ethan shook his head. "I need to talk to Catie and Brenna before I head out."

"Still upstairs."

Eliza leaned back and gave Ethan one of her studied stares. Ethan looked away because he knew that one of his sister's looks could lead to a mountain of confessions and not from her.

Ramsey mentioned to Ethan before he left the room, "I'll be heading into town after dawn to check in on Cyrus."

"I'll check with you before I head back out."

Ethan found his wife and Catie playing with Jacob in the nursery. "You're all up early."

Brenna held out her hands for Ethan to help her up off the

quilt they'd laid on the rug. "Jacob woke a few minutes after you left. You weren't the only one who couldn't sleep."

"So it would seem." Ethan glanced down at Catie. "I have to ride out for a few hours, but when I get back, I'd like to have a few words with you, Catie."

Catie barely glanced up from the toy train she rolled in front of Jacob. "What's going to happen to Cyrus?"

Ethan crouched low until he could look Catie in the eyes. "It's not up to me what happens to him. Does he frighten you?"

Catie looked up at him, her bright eyes filled with fear. "I don't want him to hurt my pa."

"He won't, I promise." Ethan held his hand out to ruffle Jacob's hair, but his eyes remained focused on Catie. When she said nothing more, he rose. His wife ushered him into the hallway.

"I'd like to take Catie into town today. I know there's a lot happening, but she could use the distraction, and I'd like to meet with some of the townspeople about the party. Isabelle wanted to come as well. I was going to wait until you returned, but Ramsey mentioned he was riding in today."

Ethan watched the young girl roll the toy train to Jacob and encourage him to roll it back. "I should be the one taking you into town."

Brenna cupped her husband's face in both hands. "You can't be everywhere, my love. I won't ask exactly what you'll be doing because I'll only fret, but I will ask you to be careful." Brenna welcomed the strong arms that circled her. "Do you know who hurt Ramsey?"

Ethan's pulled away and smirked. "I thought you weren't going to ask."

Brenna's lips twitched, but her efforts to hide her smile failed. "I lied."

Sober now, Ethan said, "I can speculate, but I'd rather find the man in case I'm wrong. Colton's confident he can track our unwanted visitor, and we need to try."

"Is it dangerous? No, don't answer that. Be sure to come back to me, Ethan."

"Always."

11

Ethan no longer felt the bitter cold. An hour after they rode away from the ranch, they lost the trail. Determined not to give up, he and Colton narrowed down the possibilities. If the attacker continued in the general direction he'd taken since leaving the ranch, he could only be going to one of two places—the old trappers cabin or farther north to Desperate Creek. One of those places held fond memories for Ethan, the other they should have burned to ash after Andrew's kidnapping.

The memories were to be on the surface, waiting for an opportune time to remind Ethan not only of the destruction Nathan Hunter had caused during those years, but also how close they'd come to losing people they loved. Ethan smiled when the memory of their old housekeeper and friend, Mabel, had welcomed Brenna into the family. They still mourned her death, but she'd left behind a house filled with love. Ethan shook the thoughts from his mind and returned to the present.

"I'd wager on the cabin. It would be suicide to travel as far north as Desperate Creek in this weather."

Colton nodded. "We're not far."

Sure enough, less than a quarter mile away from the cabin, riding quietly beneath the curtain of snow-dusted pine trees, they saw the thin stream of smoke from the cabin's fireplace. Colton remained out front while Ethan crouched low and made a wide circle around the side of the cabin to where he could look into one of the windows. Empty. He pressed himself against the rough-hewn logs and moved along the cabin to the other side where he could look in the other window. Still, no one.

Ethan returned to where Colton waited. "Anything?"

Colton shook his head. "Wait here a minute." Colton stepped quietly away, but instead of going toward the cabin, he walked in the opposite direction. Ethan listened to the sounds of the forest settle around him while he kept watch on the cabin. With a fire lit, their target couldn't be too far.

Colton approached from the side, not making a sound and whispered. "A fresh set of tracks—man and horse—about fifty feet north."

They wouldn't have a lot of daylight left if they continued north.

Colton said, "It's possible this man was just looking for something to steal."

Ethan thought of Catie and where the man had stood beneath the windows. "We won't know until we find him."

Ethan and Colton ran their horses as fast as they could through the deep snow until they saw another horse and rider ahead of them. The rider bent lower against his horse's neck, but overextended and ended up in the snow and his horse continued on a short distance before stopping.

Colton saw the gun first and shouted for Ethan to keep low. The man in the snow fired three times, forcing them to return fire. Ethan and Colton shot at the ground around the man until he ran out of bullets. The culprit attempted to run, but managed only a few feet before Ethan and Colton rode up behind him. Ethan reached out and grabbed the back of the man's coat, dragging him a few feet before dropping him back in the snow.

"Don't bother to try that again." Ethan dismounted, gun in

hand, while Colton kept his rifle trained on the man. Ethan studied the other man, now covered in snow, his face wet and red from the cold. The man could have been just another stranger passing through, looking for something to steal, if it hadn't been for the eyes. Sorrowful eyes, the color of hickory, stared back at Ethan.

"You didn't have to run, and I'd wager you're the one who knocked out my brother-in-law."

The man's chest heaved as he inhaled the cold air. "You took my daughter."

"You left your daughter alone to fend for herself! She was half-starved and driven from your home. She's lucky it was us who found her and not someone else. Where were you, Joseph?"

The man's eyes widened. "She told you about me?"

"She mentioned your name, but Cyrus told us the rest, or at least his version of the truth."

"You haven't got no right to keep her from me."

Ethan stepped closer and lowered his voice to a whisper. "As far as I'm concerned, you gave up your rights when you left her, but that's for a judge to decide." Ethan nodded to Colton who fetched Joseph's horse. "Mount up."

Joseph hesitated, then pulled himself up to the saddle without argument. He didn't take his eyes off Ethan while Colton tied the man's hands behind him. "How am I supposed to ride like this?"

"Carefully," Ethan said before he swung up on his stallion.

Catie stared at the narrow shelf of books in the general store and thought of her father. He didn't know how to read well, and he didn't do right by her most of the time, but she couldn't believe he was the bad man her uncle Cyrus claimed. He borrowed a book for her once called *Robinson Crusoe*. She hadn't been able to read more than a few chapters before her father used it as fuel for the fire when the wood she'd gathered was too damp.

The books lining the shelf gleamed and exuded a scent that pulled her in and had her reaching out to touch one of the smooth spines. They were newer than the books in the Gallagher's library, and she wondered what it would be like to read from freshly printed pages.

"Have you chosen one, Catie?"

Brenna stepped up beside her, a basket on her arm. She reached out and pulled a volume from the shelf. "This was one of my father's favorite books. It's a book of adventures written by a clever man from Scotland, my own country. Pirates and parrots and daring feats." Brenna handed the book to Catie. "Every child should have a copy of their own *Treasure Island*."

Catie watched as Brenna walked away to speak with Isabelle and the shopkeeper. Her eyes drifted downward to gaze upon the book. She allowed herself that moment of wonder and smiled. It felt good to smile for no reason other than she was happy. Catie didn't know how long it would last, but she was tired of fearing her future. She longed to believe Ethan and Brenna when they said everything would be all right.

Brenna smiled and waved her over to the counter. When Catie hesitated to place the book on the counter, Loren leaned down and rested his arms on the wood. "That's a good one you've picked. You go right ahead and keep hold of it."

Catie pulled the book against her body and held it close. She found another smile within herself and offered it to the shopkeeper as she walked with Brenna and Isabelle from the store.

When they arrived back at the ranch, Brenna asked Catie to join her in the kitchen where Ben laid their parcels. Catie still clung to the book Brenna had purchased for her, but the real surprise came when Brenna untied the strings around the brown paper parcels. A dress, too small for Brenna, was unfolded and draped over the back of a chair. Another dress, a white nightgown, and soft white stockings followed. The other package was unwrapped and revealed a long coat that looked a little like the one Brenna wore.

"They'll need to be taken in a little here and there, and perhaps the hem raised a bit. The coat needs more work, but between all of us we can manage." Brenna held the first dress up and motioned Catie over. In a daze, the young girl stepped toward Brenna and held out her hand to finger the soft cloth. She raised questioning eyes, and Brenna responded with a smile and gentle nod. "They're yours. I wanted them to be a surprise, but . . ."

Catie's eyes glistened.

"It's all they had close to your size."

"They're so pretty." Catie's bright, brown eyes lost a few of their shadows. "I get to keep them?"

Brenna had never known what it was to live without nice clothes, plenty to eat, and a safe home, and it pained her to know this child had gone without any of these for far too long. "Yes, you get to keep them. You'll also need something special for the Christmas party in town. I've ordered a holiday dress from Denver that should be here before the party. "

Elizabeth and Amanda strolled into the kitchen, the younger holding Jacob. "Did I hear something about a Christmas party?" Elizabeth asked.

"You did, indeed." Brenna handed the dress to Catie so she could hold it up and reached out to welcome her son. "Thank you for looking after him today, Amanda."

"It was my pleasure. I don't get nearly enough time with the little man. So, you talked to some of the people in town about the party?"

"We did. Loren's wife, Joanna, is especially anxious to help out," Isabelle answered walking in from the other room with Andrew. "She's going to tell everyone who walks into the store, and we hope to gain a few volunteers from her efforts."

Brenna shifted Jacob from one hip to the other before sitting down at the table. "Loren loved the idea and said it was about time the town had a Christmas celebration all together, and he was sorry he hadn't thought of it himself. He's donating candles for the tree and a few other odds and ends. We ordered what else we needed. Isabelle spoke with Tilly at the café, and she'll be helping with the food." Brenna looked up at her grandmother. "I told her you'd have some ideas about that."

Elizabeth replied with a gleeful smile. "I do. I'll have one of the young men drive me into town to visit with her."

"Oh, Tilly said she would come here."

Elizabeth waved the idea away. "Nonsense. She has a café to run, and I could use a bit of socializing. I heard from Eliza that Mrs. Jenkins said the ladies in town planned on starting a quilting circle."

Brenna watched with fondness as Catie continued to stroke the material of her new clothes. "Catie, dear. Why don't you take those upstairs and try them on? We'll see what needs hemming."

Elizabeth leaned forward. "New clothes? Well, aren't those pretty."

Catie smiled at the women, gathered up the clothes, and in a brave move, leaned in and pressed a kiss to Brenna's cheek. She whispered an equally giddy and tearful "thank you" in Brenna's ear before leaving the room.

Elizabeth thanked Amanda for the hot cup of tea, but Elizabeth was looking at her granddaughter. "You bought the girl new clothes."

"She needed them."

"I agree. Won't be able to do much hunting in them, though," Elizabeth said with a wry grin.

Brenna released a melodious laugh as she remembered Catie telling them about her hunting prowess and pictured her carrying a rifle in her new dress. Such bravado in a young woman, but she believed that any child who managed to survive for so long on her own could do all that Catie claimed.

Brenna sobered. "I'll admit that we started out wanting this celebration for the town, but now I'm doing it more for Catie. I want this to be a Christmas she'll never forget."

"It will be," Isabelle assured her. "We'll need to recruit the men to find us a tree, and soon. With everything else going on, I feel guilty asking."

"Don't," Brenna said. "There is a lot happening, but this celebration is important for everyone, including the town. We have more and more families moving into the area with hardly a possession to their name. Isabelle and I met a woman our age from Ireland. Rosaleen Cleary, her husband, and their young son arrived last week, though how they managed in this weather is a miracle. It's for them, too, that we press forward with our plan."

Ethan and Colton made it back to the ranch without incident, but the sun had already began its descent. They dismounted, and then Ethan untied the ropes from Joseph's wrists so he could climb down from his horse. "Hands in front."

Joseph glared at Ethan but held his hands out as told. Once he was secured again, Ethan half-dragged Joseph to the stable while Colton followed behind with the horses. They weren't inside five minutes when Gabriel burst in.

"You found him."

Ethan nodded. "North of the trappers' cabin." He pushed Joseph down onto a bench. "Don't move." Ethan motioned for his brother to follow him. They moved far enough way to not be overhead. "Is Brenna back from town?"

Gabriel nodded. "They arrived about an hour ago. Ben and Jake rode back with them, and Ramsey stayed behind to look after Cyrus. Who is he?"

Ethan looked over at Joseph. "Catie's father, Joseph Carr."

"Has he said anything useful?"

"Not yet. We'll lose light soon, but I'm going to take him into town tonight so he can join Cyrus in jail. If Joseph won't talk to us, perhaps proximity to his brother will encourage him."

"You should stay here. I'll go." Gabriel leaned against one of the stall doors. "I get why you want to be the one to handle this. Catie's become special to you and Brenna—I get that. What you need to understand is that Catie matters to all of us, and you don't have to do everything yourself."

Ethan slowly exhaled and rubbed a hand over his face, still unused to the short beard he'd grown for the winter. "I appreciate that, and I could use some time with Brenna and Jacob as well. Take Colton with you."

By the time Ethan found his way back to the house, he saw only Amanda and Isabelle in the kitchen enjoying a cup of tea. Amanda quickly stood, but he held up a hand. "No need to wait on me."

"Brenna asked me to fix a plate of dinner for you. It's still warm in the oven."

"I'll get it, thank you." With the oven glove, Ethan removed the plate of sliced beef and baked potatoes from the oven. "Do you mind if I join you ladies?"

"We'd be happy for the company," Isabelle said. "Brenna retired early."

Ethan's hand holding a fork covered with potato paused halfway to his mouth.

"She's fine," Isabelle reassured him. "She just tires easily these days."

Ethan set the fork down, stared up at the ceiling, and thought of his wife. "How did the ride into town go?"

"A success. Gabriel volunteered you and a couple of the other men to cut down and transport the large tree to town. Wasn't that nice of him?"

Ethan grinned and continued eating. "You can count on me for any help needed. I'll check with the men and work out a shift schedule that allows everyone to lend a hand." Ethan finished his meal while Isabelle and Gabriel told them about who volunteered and what each person would be doing to get ready for the celebration. He carried his empty plate to the counter, intent on heading up to check in on Brenna when Amanda drew his attention.

Amanda asked, "I did want to speak with you and Brenna about something."

Ethan turned and leaned against the washbasin. "Do you want to wait until Brenna and I are together?"

"I think it might be best if I speak with you first. Brenna needs her rest." Amanda set her cup aside and rose so she could better look at Ethan. "I'd like to spend a few nights a week in town. Many families have fallen on hard times, especially those who came here counting on the train to follow." Amanda glanced quickly at Isabelle and then looked back to Ethan. "The reverend is helping who he can, and he's had some generous donations of food and other staples, but I'd like to help out a few days a week—three at most—watching some of the younger children or helping the reverend where I can."

"Amanda." Isabelle's eyes glistened. "That's incredibly generous of you."

"I had no one when I arrived here, and all of you gave me a home, a purpose, and a family. I can't give much, but I can give back some of my time."

Ethan studied Amanda, in awe of her charitable spirit. His family gave money and time when they could, but most people who come to a place like Montana aren't looking for handouts, nor would they accept them. Pride has led to lean winters and near-starvations, and only the most desperate accepted charity. "You don't have to ask us, Amanda. Your kindness does you justice. How will you convince these families to let you help, not just with your time, but with provisions?"

"It's true, they don't want charity, but the reverend said he has an idea about that. I'll stay at the boarding house, but I'm afraid I'll need to ask for a ride to and from town or perhaps borrow a horse."

Ethan shook his head but was quick to add, "One or two of us from the ranch will be going into town most days before Christmas, so we'll see you there and back. It will be safer than horseback with the days so short. We'll work something out after the holidays. And, there's no need to stay at the boarding house. The cottage is empty, and we'd be pleased if you'd stay there."

"That's generous of you. Thank you."

Ethan settled his arms on Amanda's shoulders, a gesture he normally reserved for his sister. "You're a part of this family, and we all do our part. You make us very proud," he said with a warm smile.

Ethan offered his good night and left Amanda and Isabelle in the kitchen discussing Amanda's plans. He knew the other women in the house would sew and bake, but he hoped whatever the reverend had planned, worked. A few of the men from town had been hired to help Gabriel build his house, but now that it was almost finished, most of those men wouldn't have any other source of income through the winter. The other smaller ranches in the area wouldn't be hiring on again until spring. They couldn't create jobs where there were none, and when it came to the ranch, the Gallaghers didn't hire just anyone. Most of the cowhands out of work simply moved on, but those with families who wanted to make the area their home, had a more difficult time finding jobs.

His father once told him that no one could solve the problems in the world, and no matter how one tried, there would always be someone else in need. The weight bearing down on Ethan's mind evaporated when he reached the top of the stairs. A beautiful voice carried down the hall, and Ethan walked toward the nursery to spend a few minutes alone with his wife and son. He pushed the door slowly inward and froze.

Ethan stared at the fluttering curtains and the echo of a lullaby from his own childhood. He walked cautiously into the room, sensing his son was not in danger. As before, Jacob breathed softly as he slept in peace. Another sense, this one deeper and more familiar, coursed around Ethan as he stood by the crib in his son's nursery. Moonlight cast delicate rays over Jacob's face. Ethan's eyes told them they were alone in the room, but the innermost part of a person that believed in the unknown and unseen, alerted him to the presence of another.

Ethan settled himself into the vacant rocking chair and with a hand on his son's crib, he rested his eyes and waited.

"Ethan?"

He blinked and awoke immediately. "Brenna?" Ethan looked around the dimly lit room. Dawn was approaching and the rim of the eastern mountains glowed with the promise of a sunrise that would soon disappear into the waiting snow clouds.

Brenna knelt on the rug at his feet, her hands resting on his legs. "Have you been in here all night?"

It only took a second to shake away any lingering grogginess. "When I came upstairs last night, I heard you—or thought I did—singing to Jacob. No one was in here, so you're not the only one hearing things now."

Brenna rose and leaned over Jacob's crib where he continued to sleep soundly. "He's slept better in the past two weeks than he ever has. There's no danger to him, so whatever we're imagining,

I'm pleased if it brings a beautiful, sleepy smile to Jacob's lips." She held out her hand which Ethan promptly grasped before rising. "I missed you last night."

Ethan enfolded her in his arms. "Not as much as I missed you. How is Catie?"

"Restless. I sense that she's not used to remaining inside for long, much like three siblings I know." Brenna's brow rose with her grin.

"She reminds me of Eliza at that age."

"How so?"

"A free spirit trapped inside someone who shirks society's rules. Eliza knows this, and it won't help to tell her I told you, but she could outshoot and outride me and Gabriel for a long time. Mother gave up when Eliza was about Catie's age. She did her best to teach cooking and sewing and whatever else a young girl learns, but Eliza was happiest on the back of a horse." Ethan considered his words as though he just realized the truth behind them. He nor Brenna knew what to do with a girl like Catie except to love her unconditionally. Ethan could expand upon her education of riding, shooting, and ranching while Brenna educate her in the more ladylike pursuits, but there was another Gallagher who could understand Catie better than any of them.

Ethan didn't know what a judge would say about Catie and worried what would happen with Joseph Carr once he was released from jail.

12

The morning sun arrived at a leisurely pace, seemingly content to hide behind a blanket of snow clouds until the last possible moment. Brenna had convinced Ethan to drive her into town after breakfast. Ethan's reluctance hadn't been voiced until they were a mile from the ranch, and Brenna confessed the reason behind her desire to visit town. He hadn't turned the wagon around, but he managed to wrest a few promises from her before they continued.

Brenna harbored no guilt—or at least not enough to speak of—because her sole concern was for Catie. It was that knowledge, she believed, which kept Ethan from carting her back to the ranch rather than drive into Briarwood. When he coaxed the horses to a stop in front of the jail, Ethan's heavy sigh accompanied a hand on Brenna's blanket-covered leg.

"Is there any way I convince you not to do this?"

"You'll be there, so there's no risk of harm coming to me. Gabriel and Colton are also inside. No woman in all of Montana will be better protected." Brenna covered her husband's hand with her own. "Besides, you told me Joseph Carr isn't a violent man."

"I *believe* he's not a violent man," Ethan clarified. "There's a difference."

"Very well. If you feel that strongly about me not going inside, then I won't."

Ethan's brow lifted, and after a few seconds, he smirked. "It's nice of you to let me believe I have a say."

Brenna leaned into Ethan and smiled beneath the gentle caress of his lips. Once he secured the horses, Ethan helped his wife down from the wagon, and with his hand pressed to the small of her back, walked beside Brenna into the jail.

Gabriel waited with hot coffee and a chair by the stove for Brenna. "I saw you drive up. To what do we owe the honor?"

Ethan hung his hat on one of the pegs by the door and accepted the cup his brother offered. "Have you managed to get anything out of Joseph yet?"

"When he isn't sleeping, he's not talking. I've been trying for hours and that's after Colton gave up last night. Now, it's possible he's not saying much because of his brother, but I don't know what good it will do for you to even try."

"Is he dangerous?" Brenna asked.

Gabriel response was a reluctant one. "I don't believe so. It's true, he injured Ramsey, but he could have done a lot worse, and he hasn't given us any trouble besides yelling at his brother. What exactly are you doing here?"

Ethan swallowed and glanced at his wife. "Brenna would like a few words with Joseph."

She was quick to add, "If he remained in irons, or whatever you do with prisoners, and then I can speak with him out here for just a few minutes."

Gabriel released a sigh and looked toward the back room just as Colton walked in through the front door carrying a heavy tray covered in a thick checkered cloth. Colton's eyes clamped down on the new arrivals, and then he continued to the desk where he set down the tray. Looking at everyone, he asked "Something happened?"

Gabriel's lips turned up into an imperceptible grin. "Brenna wishes to speak with Joseph Carr."

"That's not a good idea."

"I already told her that," Ethan said.

"Joseph does need to eat," Colton said glancing between Brenna and Ethan. "And Cyrus's company would sour anyone's appetite."

Gabriel gave up and disappeared with the keys into the back room.

"You're displeased," Brenna said.

Colton looked up from the tray where he'd been unstacking the plates of food. "No, but surprised. What's so important to bring you over here, and why do you think he'll speak with you?" Colton glanced to Ethan, but his boss merely shrugged and grinned, leaving Colton to wonder.

"I don't believe I can explain it in a way that will satisfy anyone. Suffice it to say, I'm thinking only of Catie, and a man like Joseph Carr is more likely to speak with someone who's of no threat to him."

Gabriel emerged from the back room with Jospeh. Brenna remained sitting, though she faced Catie's father. His face was gaunt like a man who hadn't eaten or slept well in months. She felt the heat from Ethan's body as he stood behind her, one hand on her shoulder.

"Mr. Carr."

He narrowed his eyes, eyes the same shape and color as Catie's. "Who the hell are you?"

Gabriel smacked Joseph on the back of his head. "Show the lady respect."

"I'm Brenna Gallagher. I believe you've already met my husband."

Joseph looked to Ethan with a sneer, and then to the others, but no one offered an explanation.

Gabriel said, "Sit here at the desk and eat your breakfast. It's your only respite from Cyrus until the deputies come for him."

Joseph accepted the food and ate with relish. Neither Colton nor Gabriel touched their meal. Gabriel carried one of the plates to the back room and returned a moment later. His exit from the cells was followed by a clatter. "Guess Cyrus wasn't hungry."

"Cyrus was always stupid," Joseph said between bites that had now slowed a little.

Gabriel caught Brenna's eye and nodded to Joseph. In silent words he was telling her to say what she wanted to say because her time was running out.

"Mr. Carr," Brenna began, "I'd like to ask you about Catie."

Joseph's hand stopped before the fork reached his mouth. "I ain't saying nothing."

Undaunted, Brenna continued. "You know Catie is staying with us, and it's only her welfare which brings me here today. She's an incredibly bright and intelligent girl, Mr. Carr, and were she my daughter—"

"She ain't yours."

Brenna held Ethan in place with a gentle touch to the hand still on her shoulder. Antagonizing Joseph would thwart her efforts. "No, she's yours. She looks up to you and doesn't understand why you left. Catie deserves answers, but right now I'm most concerned about what's going to happen to her."

Joseph kept his eyes averted and resumed eating, but he did say, "Good reader."

With astounding patience, Brenna replied, "Yes, she seems eager to learn. My sister-in-law is a schoolteacher, and Catie has sat in on several lessons. Your daughter has great potential."

Brenna held the rapt attention of all three men and soldiered on. "I realize she may not be with us long, but I would like your permission to have her studies continued until after the holidays. An education to take with her when she moves away."

Joseph's fork clattered to his plate. "She ain't going anywhere."

Ethan's hand squeezed her shoulder, a warning that she was running out of time before Ethan took over the discussion. She hurried and said, "If you're sent away to prison, then Catie will have no family left, and her fate will be at the mercy of a judge. I'd like her to be well prepared for whatever school she may attend after Christmas."

The words twisted Brenna's insides, and had she not felt the rise and fall of her own chest, she'd think her heart had stopped. As painful as the words had been to say, they elicited the response she'd wanted.

Joseph twisted in the chair to look up at Gabriel. "That true? They going to take my girl away?"

Brenna was prepared to silently plead with the men not to detract her efforts, but they had caught on to her plan.

"It's possible. We'd like to help her out and keep her on at the ranch instead of sending her away to an orphanage, but my husband tells me that's up to a judge."

"What do I got to do to keep my girl?"

Brenna felt the tension leave her husband before he said, "You have to talk to us, tell us what happened, and why you abandoned her."

"I didn't have no choice about leaving Catie. She's a strong girl and smart, too. I knew she'd get along better without me."

"That's not good enough," Colton said from his position behind Joseph. "She had to steal food to survive and would have frozen had she not stumbled upon one of the Gallaghers' line shacks. Worse, what if Cyrus and his friends, or a drifter, had found her first?"

Joseph's face blanched. "She wasn't hurt none, was she?"

"No," Gabriel said. "Why not take her with you?"

"Cyrus."

"That didn't stop him from coming after her to get to you." Gabriel's voice had taken on a sharp edge. "What does Cyrus want?"

Joseph shifted in his seat, remaining silent.

It was Brenna's turn again. "Mr. Carr. I'm a mother, so I can understand the lengths and depths to which a parent might go to protect their child. I see how much you love Catie, but loving a child means doing whatever you must to keep her safe with no regard for yourself. You owe it to your daughter to do right by her."

Joseph spoke directly to Brenna this time. "If something happens to me, Catie will be taken away."

"Is something going to happen to you, Mr. Carr?" Ethan asked.

Joseph remained silent for a full minute, long enough for Brenna to wonder if she'd pushed him too far, but then he spoke. "Cyrus robbed a train down Bozeman way a few months back. It was carrying payroll for the miners in Butte."

Gabriel nodded. "We know, that's why he's being transferred to Bozeman."

"Cyrus thinks I stole the money."

A quick glance passed between the three men, and Brenna wished she knew what they were thinking.

Colton asked, "Did you steal the money?"

"I ain't no thief." Joseph pushed away his cleaned-off plate. "A judge can't take Catie away if I ain't done nothing wrong."

Gabriel crossed his arms and stared down at Joseph. "You left her alone, and a judge can take her away for that. Besides, Cyrus wouldn't have come after her if he didn't believe you had the money."

Joseph ignored Gabriel and turned to Brenna. "You sure my girl is looked after?"

With the compassion of a mother, Brenna smiled at Joseph.

"She is, and you have my promise she will continue to be safe and looked after."

Joseph pushed away from the desk and rose to look Gabriel in the eye, though he stood a couple of inches shorter. "Cyrus ain't the only one who took that money. He's got a partner."

"He rode with two men," Gabriel said.

Joseph shook his head. "No, this partner does the telling and Cyrus does the thieving. You promise my girl is safe out there at your ranch? If I tell you what else I know, Cyrus's partner is going to come for my girl if he can't get me."

Gabriel said, "I promise."

Joseph nodded once. "Cyrus gave me the stolen money for safekeeping seeing as how no one saw me, but I ain't saying anything else. I want to go back to my cell now."

He stepped around from the back of the desk and stepped toward Brenna. Gabriel put his arm out to block him, and Ethan stepped in front of his wife. Brenna rose and stood beside Ethan, a hand on his arm. Joseph handed Ethan a small pendant, and after a moment, he passed it to Brenna.

"Will you give that to Catie?" Joseph asked.

The small, silver, oval necklace was a locket. Brenna pressed the latch and opened it. Inside was a likeness of Catie when she was younger. On the other side, a picture of a young woman who no doubt was the face of Catie's future. "Her mother?"

Joseph nodded, his eyes on the locket. "You teach her what you can. She ought to be better than her pa." He looked to Gabriel. "You write it out, and I'll put my name to it. I don't want Catie going to no orphanage."

"Mr. Carr, wait."

Joseph turned halfway across the room.

"How old is Catie?"

"Fourteen years old this year. I told her so myself." He considered for a long moment, his face going pale, his mouth agape. "She'd be thirteen years now. I didn't think . . ."

Brenna wondered if Catie would be thrilled or disappointed that she'd gained another year of life. "And her birthday?"

Joseph scratched his beard and looked away. "I wasn't there for Catie's birth. Her ma told me a year after Catie was born. September is her birthday. That's it. I'm sure that's when I told her." Without prodding or guidance, he walked to the door Colton had opened and voluntarily returned to his cell.

"You're worthless; nothing," Cyrus yelled and cursed at his brother. The bars barely rattled beneath his heavy grip. "You better not have told them nothing."

"He didn't say anything, Cyrus," Gabriel said. "Now do everyone a huge favor and shut up until the deputies from Bozeman arrive."

Gabriel closed the door, Cyrus shouting all the while. "I can't believe it, Brenna. You got him to talk."

"I don't know if it did much good," Brenna replied. "Something about the way he returned to his cell, it's as though he's given up." She ran her thumb over the locket and wondered if Catie even remembered her mother. Catie would have the life she deserved, and by God, she would have a birthday party next September. "What will happen to him?"

It was Ethan who, after some hesitation, said, "He participated in the robbery. They might be lenient if he confesses and tells them where to find the money, but there's no guarantee."

The single shout was cut off by silence and what sounded like a struggle against the bars. Gabriel and Colton rushed into the back room, leaving Ethan with Brenna to watch on in shock at what she witnessed through the open door. Joseph's arms were through the bars, one of them pressed against Cyrus's neck. The pressure was enough to turn Cyrus's face a shade of dark red as Joseph tugged his brother tighter against the bars. Gabriel unlocked the cell that housed Cyrus and tossed the keys to Colton so he could get into Joseph's cell, but they were both too late. Ethan asked his wife to remain in the office while he helped Colton. Cyrus fell to the ground when Colton and Ethan yanked Joseph away from the bars.

"He ain't never going to hurt my girl again."

Gabriel held Cyrus up and felt for a pulse. He looked through the bars at Joseph. "He's not dead."

Colton locked Joseph's cell back up and hurried from the jailhouse. Brenna lowered the hand she had pressed to her chest and eased closer until she stood in the doorway.

"You don't want to be back here," Gabriel called out.

Ethan swore and left the cell to join his wife, but instead of taking Gabriel's advice or the urgings of her husband, Brenna's eyes focused on Joseph. "Why?"

"He can't hurt Catie again. I won't let him. I've done that enough myself."

Brenna watched Joseph as his eyes shifted to his brother. Sadness and anger blended together with regret. He stepped toward the bars. "I know I didn't deserve a girl as special as Catie. I didn't deserve her ma, either, but I loved 'em both, even if I didn't do right by them. Catie's ma didn't do right by her either." To Gabriel he said, "You got a judge here in this town?"

"No, but we have a former U.S. Marshal. You have something more to say?"

Joseph nodded and stared back down at his brother. "Bring the marshal here. I'll say it to him."

13

Catie rode free over the snowy earth, allowing the mare to carry her over familiar ground. Eliza remembered the freedom and sheer wonder she experienced when she first galloped through the snow. The young girl may be new to a saddle, but she was a natural. Eliza imagined what she'd be capable of with a little practice. Catie's laughter rushed with the wind, and despite her red face from the cold and the light snow falling down, the girl's face revealed incomparable joy.

Ethan had started to ask some odd questions about what it was like for Eliza growing up. Odd, because he'd grown up beside her, but when he brought up Catie, Eliza realized her brother's motives. Eliza and Ramsey needed to get back to their ranch, so they volunteered to take Catie with them. The breeding facility wouldn't be completed until spring, but they had plenty to keep them busy until then. Nathan Hunter's herd had come with the ranch but had been combined with the Hawk's Peak herd when the family had the boundaries redrawn to encompass both ranches. Eliza preferred horses to cattle, and she saw that same love in Catie.

The mare slowed when it circled back to Ramsey and Eliza. "You're a natural out there," Ramsey said.

"This is different from the first time. I was free, but also a little scared, and then those men chased us." Catie's smile faltered for a slight second. "But it's the most wonderful thing, isn't it?"

"It's my favorite thing." Eliza glanced at her husband, "Well, second favorite thing."

Catie leaned forward and ran her hand along the neck of the spotted gray mare. "Is it true you were a lawman, Mr. Cameron?"

"You can call me Ramsey, and yes, for a short time."

"Do you know what's going to happen to me?"

Ramsey leaned on the pommel of his saddle. "What do you want to happen to you?"

No one had ever asked her that before, at least not directly. Ethan and Brenna promised that everything would work out, but what did she want? Would it matter to a judge if she wanted to live with the Gallaghers? Would they want her to live with them if it was permitted? Ethan and Brenna treated her better than anyone she'd ever known, but they had their own child and another baby coming. Catie was too old for people to want her, but maybe she could help people in town, perhaps get work to live on her own.

"I don't want to go away," she confessed.

Ramsey nodded and sat straight in the saddle. "Well, let's see what we can do about that." They returned to the house where Eliza pulled him aside.

"Ethan and Brenna have avoided making that girl any promises. They'd take her in a minute—any of us would—but it's not up to us. We don't even know what's going to happen with her father."

Ramsey looked over his wife's shoulder at Catie who was occupied with the mare. "I'm not making a promise. Brenna and Ethan went to speak with Joseph, and perhaps they've come to an arrangement. In the meantime, there's a judge in Wyoming who owes me a favor."

"He won't have jurisdiction up here."

"No, but I will provide that girl any help we can." Ramsey watched Catie remove the saddle from the mare as they'd taught her. "I grew up thinking I was an orphan, and not a day goes by when I wish I had known my parents, and then the loss was even deeper when I learned I had a sister. Brenna tells me stories about growing up in Scotland, but it's not the same thing. I wandered for years because I didn't have a home, so I understand Catie, maybe better than anyone else. She may as well be close to an orphan now, and I'll be damned if I don't do everything I can to keep her from missing out on having a family."

Eliza pulled her husband down for a kiss, lingered over his warm lips, and pulled back wearing a wide grin. "How'd I get so lucky to find you?"

Discussion about the Christmas party was well under way back at the ranch house. Catie had given a great deal of consideration to what Ramsey and Eliza had asked her. What did she want to do? The problem wasn't with the question but rather how to execute what she already knew. Catie wanted to stay at Hawk's Peak, or at least in Briarwood where she could see the Gallaghers as often as she liked. She reckoned fourteen was old enough to make up her own mind, but in the deepest part of her heart, she ached to be part of a real family.

Laughter and animated voices filled the room, drawing a secret smile from Catie as she listened to the women's plans for the celebration.

Elizabeth chimed in with her own boisterous addition to the conversation. "Amanda and I have the menu planned out, and with Tilly's help, there should be more than enough food for everyone."

"The men here will take care of cutting down and setting up the tree in town," Isabelle said. "Now we'll need volunteers to decorate it, though with what I'm not yet certain. Because it's outside, the usual ornaments won't suffice."

"We'll come up with something," Amanda said.

Brenna lowered her teacup and smiled at her son's laughter. "You have a way with him, Catie." To the others she said, "We ordered ribbons from Loren while we were in town." Catie followed their conversation yet remained silent until Brenna asked her a question. "What do you think should go on the tree, Catie?"

Catie paused in her play with Jacob and raised her eyes to Brenna before casting a quick glance to each person in the room. "I'm not sure."

Catie had never decorated a Christmas tree and certainly not a grand one outdoors. She remembered a colorful tree covered with bright round balls and sparkling lights in the window of a house she and her father passed two winters ago.

Now at the center of attention, Catie thought back to that tree in the window and shrugged. "Maybe my ma's locket or a doll if I knew how to make one. Can those go on a tree?"

"They certainly can." Brenna mulled a moment and then said, "Why don't we ask everyone to bring one item to place on the tree on Christmas day. Something special to them that tells a story of their lives and perhaps of this town."

"A delightful idea." Amanda looked to Catie. "And I can show you how to make a doll if you'd like. You already know how to stitch, so it will be simple enough."

Catie beamed. "Can I have it done by Christmas Eve?"

"I don't see why not."

One by one the women shared their ideas for what could go on the tree, all the while Catie watched each of them with an excitement similar to the moment when Brenna showed her the shelves of books. They included her, asked her opinion, and treated her as though she'd always been in their lives. Catie belonged, and whether her mind fully accepted that yet, her heart already knew.

14

Two days late, the deputies arrived with an official order of transfer from Sheriff Johnson in Bozeman, though neither of them appeared happy to be on the errand. One of the men stood almost as tall as Gabriel and the other six inches shorter. Without a spur line into Briarwood, they would have traveled by horse or wagon, a feat Gabriel wouldn't have wanted to undertake in the winter. The road out of Briarwood was traveled just enough to keep it semi-clear, but Gabriel didn't trust Cyrus on the back of his own horse.

Gabriel poured each of the men a cup of coffee from the pot warming over the small woodstove. "I don't suppose you brought a wagon with you."

The tall, lanky one introduced himself as Deputy Carlson and thanked Gabriel for the coffee. He drank deeply before answering. "Sheriff Johnson wanted me and Deputy Peterson here to make better time than a wagon would allow."

Deputy Peterson looked like he could wrestle a bull and come out the victor. "We brought an extra horse for the prisoner."

Gabriel set his own mug down and crossed his arms as he leaned against the desk. "I'd advise against that with this one. If you put Cyrus Carr on the back of a horse, he'll find a way to get loose. Trussed up in the back of wagon is the best way. At least then if he tries to jump out, he'll break something in the fall." Gabriel pointed across the street. "I'll get you a wagon from livery, we can hook up your horses, and you'll have an easier trip back with your prisoner."

Deputy Carlson shrugged and shook his head. "Sheriff wants us back in Bozeman with Carr. He's got a judge and jury ready for a trial as soon as we arrive, and then it's off to Deer Lodge for the prisoner where he becomes Warden Conley's problem."

Tried and sentenced before he stepped foot into a courtroom. Gabriel marveled at the justice, or lack thereof, even as he wondered how these men could be so certain of the trial's outcome. He wouldn't concern himself much with Cyrus when they still had to figure out what to do with Joseph.

Gabriel removed the cell keys from the top drawer of the desk and told the deputies to follow him. "I'd still recommend a wagon, but either way, I'm glad he's leaving." Gabriel unlocked Cyrus's cell and stepped aside to let Deputy Peterson inside where he cuffed Cyrus.

"He's a rowdy one," Deputy Carlson commented under his breath, and Gabriel chose to ignore the sarcasm. Cyrus was quiet now after what Joseph had done to him. They had called over Doc Brody to look at him. Doc assured Gabriel that Cyrus would be fine, but his throat suffered some damage and he might not be able to talk for a few days. Cyrus looked up at Gabriel as the deputy maneuvered Cyrus out of the cell. Eyes, cold and dead as the frozen earth beneath the winter snow passed over Gabriel and then flicked to Joseph. The message was clear.

"Just get him out of here." Gabriel closed the cell and waited until they'd walked into the front room before saying to Joseph, "I'll be back to talk in a minute, and you better have more to say."

Gabriel joined the others in the front office, closing the door behind him. Deputy Carlson nodded toward the back room.

"What's that one in for?"

Grateful Cyrus couldn't speak, Gabriel obfuscated. "Minor assault and resisting arrest. Nothing that warrants a trial since the man he assaulted won't be pressing charges."

Deputy Peterson grinned and said, "Just teaching him a lesson, then."

"Something like that." Gabriel's gaze never left Cyrus as he was carted away by the deputies, heaved onto the back of a horse, and his hands tied to the pommel. Deputy Carlson covered Cyrus's shoulders with a thick blanket and tied a rope around his middle. At least they weren't complete fools, Gabriel thought.

When they'd ridden away, Gabriel stood at the window a few minutes longer watching the townsfolk go about their business. He noticed more homes had small trees in their windows and wreaths adorned in ribbons hanging from front doors or porch railings. The Christmas spirit was alive and thriving in Briarwood.

Gabriel's gaze trailed down the road to a modest house at the end of the street. It had been empty for three weeks. The young family who had moved to the territory hoping to farm on a small plot of land had lost their home to the bank and relocated to Denver. Their story was unfortunate, though not unique. Most homesteaders who couldn't make it didn't last long enough to get to know anyone in town or send their children to school. The people of Briarwood were there to help in any way they could, but the reality was, if a person couldn't make it on their own, they had no business in the more remote areas of the West.

Then again, he thought, not everyone had a choice. People like Catie who made the best out of the circumstances life had dealt them, were the exception. Children had no choice except to follow a parent like Joseph Carr, who would leave and force them to survive on their own or an orphanage. Neither option was good enough for Catherine Rose.

Gabriel sighed and pushed away from the window. He'd given Joseph enough time.

Catie gently pulled on the reins the way Eliza had taught her and stopped the horse in front of the house. They'd ridden to Eliza and Ramsey's home and then back again to the main ranch, and Catie had done it all on her own. She now dismounted from the mare like a girl who'd been riding horses her entire life. She landed on the frosted ground with a gentle thud and turned to grin at Eliza. "I did it."

"You certainly did."

Ramsey stepped up behind her and gently squeezed her shoulder. "You did well, Catie." He leaned in to kiss his wife before securing his own horse to the post. "I need to find Ethan."

Eliza nodded. "You go ahead. Catie and I are going inside to tell everyone we have a new horsemaster in the family." They realized the implication of what she had just said, and though it had slipped from loose lips, Eliza stood by her words. She had spent half of the night awake and kept coming around to the same solution—one way or another, Catie would be a part of Hawk's Peak. Though neither of them had said it, she believed Brenna and Ethan felt the same way.

Ramsey smoothly eased them out of the awkwardness by grinning and saying to Catie, "Make sure they save me some of whatever smells so heavenly." He cast an encouraging glance to his wife and headed toward one of the ranch hands at the corrals.

Ramsey found Ethan in the stable removing the saddle from his stallion. "Calling it quits already?"

Ethan hoisted the saddle onto the wooden rack mounted to the wall. "Hardly. I'm giving this guy a break and taking one of the green broke stallions into town. Glad you found me because I need to ask you to come along."

Ramsey ran his hand along the back of the coal-black stallion. "Has something happened?"

"Brenna managed to get Joseph Carr to talk."

"What was she doing talking to him?"

"In a moment of weakness, I might have agreed to it." Ethan shrugged. "Give yourself a little more time and see how well you say no to Eliza."

Ramsey feigned surprise. "I'm allowed to say 'no' to her?"

Ethan grinned as he saddled the black and white Quarter Horse. "We can try. As for Brenna speaking to Joseph, it turned out she was right. Joseph wants to speak to a lawman, and you're the closest we have. He isn't aware that the former marshal is also the man he almost killed."

"I won't hold that against him." Ramsey studied the lines of the horse. "Is this one you bred?"

Ethan cinched the saddle and rubbed the horse's neck. "Bred my black with one of the mustangs four years back. Eliza has been training this one in nice and slow. So far he's shaping out to be a good breeding prospect for the new herd."

"He has good genes," Ramsey remarked.

"Good temperament, too." Ethan checked the fittings and turned to Ramsey. "How did Catie enjoy the ride this afternoon?"

"She loved it. I knew when we first took her out that she was a natural. She and Eliza are in the house now. Listen, Ethan, if it turns out Catie can stay on at the ranch, what are your plans?"

Ethan smoothed his hand over the horse's forehead, lifting the black mane from beneath the leather strap of the bridle. "Brenna loves the girl—we all do—but I want what's best for her."

"She'll stay with you and Brenna, won't she?"

"I hope so, why?"

"She reminds me of Eliza. I imagine her at that age . . ."

Ethan grinned. "I thought the same thing, and Catie's just as resilient. One obstacle at a time, though. First, we need to find out what Joseph Carr knows and then get a judge to make a decision about Catie."

"It would be easier if Joseph gave his consent for Catie to remain with us."

Ethan's breath hitched. That's exactly what he hoped Joseph would do, but he'd avoided saying it aloud just in case it didn't happen. "He as much said he would and told us to write it out so he can sign the papers."

"Do you believe he will?"

"I can see he loves his daughter, in his own way. I hope he follows through, but right now, we need him to talk. If he did nothing wrong, we can't hold him and he can take his daughter."

Ramsey walked alongside the young stallion as Ethan led him outside. "I might be able to help."

Dusk arrived as Ethan and Ramsey rode into town. They waited for news from the Boston lawyer, and Ramsey was confident that his friend, the judge in Wyoming, could recommend a course of action. But unless Joseph was deemed unfit, or confessed to involvement with the train robbery, there was nothing any of them could do to prevent him from taking Catie.

Ramsey thought Ethan would rather be at home decorating the big tree the men had helped cut down that morning for the house. Work on the ranch didn't stop, even for the holidays, but this was one of the first Christmases in years with relatively little conflict, and they all intended to spend as much time with family as possible.

He and Ramsey walked into the quiet jail. "Gabe?"

Gabriel sauntered from the back room and raised his cup. "I'm glad to see you, Ramsey. Joseph won't say a word. I swear, Brenna has a magic way about her because I can't get him to talk."

Ramsey helped himself to the coffee and offered a cup to Ethan who declined. "He wants to speak to the former marshal, but is he aware that I'm not an active marshal?"

"You're still deputized, aren't you?"

"After a fashion. Does he know that?"

Gabriel shook his head. "He does not."

Ethan kept his hat and coat on when Ramsey removed his. "I need to check in at the telegraph office before they close, but I'll be back soon."

"We're not going anywhere." Gabriel preceded Ramsey into the back room as Ethan exited out the front. "You have a visitor, Joseph."

The prisoner rose from the narrow cot and moved to the bars. "You ain't the marshal. I—"

"Knocked me out," Ramsey said dryly. "I remember. I'm the former marshal, and as close to law as we have in this town. You have something to say to me?"

"I didn't mean to hit you so hard."

Ramsey pressed against the wound on the back of his head. "Doesn't matter what you intended, now does it."

"I know where the miner's payroll is, the one Cyrus stole."

Ramsey and Gabriel exchanged a look that said neither one of them had expected the revelation. "That explains why your brother was willing to kidnap, or even kill, his own niece. Where is it?"

Joseph frantically shook his head. "What's going to happen to me if I tell you?"

Gabriel didn't think he could be more disgusted with the man. He hadn't asked what would happen to his daughter. "Depends on your part in it. You said you weren't with Cyrus when he robbed the train. Is that true?"

"I was with him, but I didn't hurt no one."

Ramsey swore and turned his back to the bars. In a low voice, he said to Gabriel, "The railroad and the mining company are going to press charges, whether he fired his gun or not."

Gabriel nodded and stepped up to the bars. "You left Catie an orphan the day you decided to break the law. What happened to her mother?"

Dejected now, Joseph said, "Ran off a long time ago. The money Cyrus wants is buried under some boards in the cabin in the woods."

"The trappers' cabin where you've been squatting?"

Joseph nodded. "That's the one. I went back for the girl, but she was already gone. I didn't know what happened to her, and that's when I searched the ranches nearby."

Gabriel's disgust blended into pity for a man who had more than he realized and now would lose everything. "You're going to prison, Joseph."

"I figured if I told you maybe I could just leave, start over with Catie in a new place."

Ramsey settled his hands on his hips and looked sideways at Joseph. "People died during that robbery, and that's not something we can overlook. We'll put in a good word for you with the judge, but that's the best we can do."

Joseph ran a hand through his grubby hair and over rough skin. "Can I see Catie one more time?"

Ramsey and Gabriel exchanged an agreeable glance. Ramsey said, "It will be Catie's decision. If she agrees, then it can be arranged."

Joseph slowly nodded and then asked the question Gabriel had been waiting to hear. "What will happen to her?"

Gabriel studied Joseph's eyes and saw true remorse. "That's up to a judge . . . and you."

Joseph's brown eyes, a mirror of his daughter's, opened wider and he stood tall in the cell wearing dirty clothes and a disheartened spirit. "Maybe there's a better way."

Ethan held two folded squares of paper in his pocket when he returned to the jail. Brenna's Boston lawyer had come through, though his news did not offer a guarantee they could keep Catie with them. The other telegram was from the circuit court judge, and the news from him was by the letter of the law. Both telegrams said essentially the same thing; the child couldn't be removed from her parent without cause. Ethan still held out hope that Joseph would do right by his daughter without interference from the law.

When Ethan stepped into the jail's front office, Ramsey and Gabriel stood by the small woodstove. "Did he tell you anything else?"

Ramsey nodded. "He'll be going to prison." Ramsey went on to repeat the conversation they'd had with Joseph and finished with, "He wants to see Catie before he's sent away."

"When will that be?"

"I have to wire the judge today, and he'll decide where and when, but I imagine it will be before Christmas."

Ethan looked to his brother. "What did you tell him about seeing Catie?"

"I told him it was up to her whether she saw him or not." Gabriel glanced over his shoulder to the cells and then back to his brother. "Catie won't be going to an orphanage."

15

Ben and Ethan came upon a quiet kitchen where only Amanda worked, humming softly to herself. A board creaked beneath Ethan's foot when he stepped over the threshold. Amanda turned, grinned, and brushed back a few strands of honey-colored hair with the back of her hand. "Finally, company! Everyone seems to be scattered this morning. Catie is with Jacob in the nursery; they're quite enamored of each other. And Eliza returned home this morning with one of the men to check on her animals." Amanda indicated a chair at the table. "We have fresh biscuits, bacon, and I can fry a couple of eggs. I pulled out a jar of canned peaches this morning."

"I'll take whatever I'm smelling," Ethan said, and Ben nodded in agreement. "Has Brenna come down yet?"

Amanda wiped the flour from her hands on her apron. "She did, but I sent her back upstairs. She looked a tad peaked." Before Amanda could assure Ethan that his wife was only tired, he hurried from the room, leaving Amanda alone with Ben.

She poured a fresh cup of coffee for him. She added a small plate of covered biscuits and a jar of raspberry preserves to the table. "Ethan may be a while. Please, have some."

"If it's no trouble." Ben eyed Amanda and took a seat at the table. He'd enjoyed many meals with the Gallaghers in this very room, but he tended to take most of his meals with the other men in the bunkhouse.

Ben sliced one of the airy biscuits, spread a generous dollop of preserves on top, and savored the first bite. "Don't tell Tilly I ever said this, but these are the best biscuits I've ever had."

Amanda smiled. "You're afraid of Tilly?"

"I'm afraid she won't cook for me again if I confess my love for another woman's cooking." Ben grinned between bites.

"Elizabeth is the real artist when it comes to food."

Ben decided there was no good response to that comment. Instead, he finished off the biscuits and then started in on the hearty breakfast Amanda set in front of him. "Are you going to join me?"

Amanda appeared to consider the offer but was saved from answering when Ethan sauntered in behind them, his worries over Brenna obviously eased. Amanda chose to pile food onto a plate and avoid Ben's penetrating gaze.

"Amanda," Ethan began. "I meant to ask you and Elizabeth if we had some foodstuff we could spare for some baskets or the like."

She turned, her gaze questioning. "Baskets?"

Ethan nodded. "Colton mentioned he was going out to visit a few of the families who live a ways out of town. He planned to go into town first for a few supplies, but the trip will take him miles out of the way."

Amanda dropped the cloth she'd used to dry a spill into a bucket and said, "There's an extra basket in the pantry for one of the families, and we can figure out some sort of bundle for the others. We have fresh loaves of bread—I can make more—and some preserves, scones, and Elizabeth's oatmeal cookies."

"Jackson added fresh cuts of venison and beef to the larder a few days ago," Ben added, referring to one of the ranch hands.

"I'll pull out the meats if you could gather those other things,"

Ethan said. "If you're sure it's all right. I don't want to make more work for you by taking away what you've already made."

"I will gladly bake a dozen loaves of bread per day if I thought it would help. I'll slice up some of Elizabeth's spice cake. If she was here, I know she'd want to add to the offering."

The wagon lumbered along what could loosely pass as a road. Two of the families lived within close distance of one another, and Amanda had spent a few minutes with each, sure to invite them to the town's Christmas celebration. Though both sets of parents appeared skeptical, the children's excitement brought them around. Colton was even quieter than Ben, though he willingly answered her questions about a type of tree or a strange noise she didn't recognize.

She knew very little of Colton or most of the men who worked at the ranch. When she offered to join Colton, she both hoped and feared Ben would also come along, but he hadn't said a word.

The last family on Colton's list was Beckert. "Do you know the Beckert family?" she asked Colton.

"I know of them. They bought a small homestead last spring." Colton navigated the team and wagon around a boulder on the lightly traveled road covered with more snow than the one to Hawk's Peak.

"It doesn't appear as though many people travel this way."

Colton pointed toward the eastern mountain ridge. "There's a small mine northeast of here. A few miners and their families live out that way, and occasionally make their way into Briarwood, but the mine supplies them with most of what they need. This road isn't traveled much otherwise."

"It would seem a lonely existence, out here for so many days of the year and no one else around."

Colton shrugged. "What some folks see as lonely, others consider quiet."

Amanda glanced sideways at her driving companion. "And which are you, Mr. Dawson, lonely or quiet?"

Colton laughed then, a deep and rich sound that surprised Amanda. "Definitely the latter, but I've grown used to life at the ranch and having people around. Can't say I'm too fond of spending much time in town, though. More and more people talk about statehood and bringing the railroad through Briarwood."

"You're against statehood and railroads?"

"Not against, just not in a hurry to see either happen around here. Changes aren't always bad, but too many of them, and the peace we have here in these mountains will disappear."

"How can it disappear?" Amanda looked around her and couldn't imagine a single thing changing.

"If it does, I hope I'm not around to see it."

Colton's eyes shifted until he was looking at the land rather than her. What did a man who'd learned to live life in these mountains do when the world threatened to close in on him? Amanda knew someday she would ask him the question, but for now, she changed the subject. "What was that bird's call I just heard?"

The pensive draw of his lips turned into a smile. "Good ear. The first one was a Cooper's Hawk. Probably has a nest nearby in the forest and warning against predators." Colton pointed to the trees on their far right and then looked around in the sky. "Up there, above the tree line."

Amanda's gaze followed where he pointed until she saw a large bird soaring beneath the clouds. "Is that an eagle?"

Colton nodded. "They're not one to make much noise, but they're formidable. They hunt in the open fields here, and more often you'll find them near rivers and lakes. You've never seen one?"

Amanda nodded. "Never this close. What a wonderful gift, to know so much about the land and its creatures."

Colton remained faced forward but answered. "A man who used to live in the mountains farther north of here taught me everything he knew—and he knew a lot—about hunting and tracking, surviving off the land."

"How old were you?"

Amanda wondered about his hesitation at such a simple answer.

"Old enough to know I wanted a different life than what I had before."

Colton glanced at her once, and then twice. After the third time, Amanda broke her own silence. "What is it?"

"Why did you volunteer to come with me today?"

Not expecting the question, Amanda replied simply, "I wanted to help. I've been here a while now, and I realized that I know so few people except in passing. I want to be more involved, to have a purpose."

Colton studied her the way he might study a fresh track in the snow to figure out where it's been and where the creature was going. "Ben is one of my closest friends."

Amanda stiffened, though she immediately disliked her own reaction. Colton continued. "I'm not one to involve myself where I'm not wanted or needed, but I get the impression he makes you uncomfortable."

"No, not at all." Amanda was quick to refute Colton's words, though they held a semblance of truth. "At least not in the way you might think."

The unexpected smile touched Colton's lips.

"It's not like that, either, Mr. Dawson."

"It's Colton, and I won't speculate," though his grin remained. Colton pointed farther up the road. "There's the

Beckert's homestead, just ahead."

Amanda turned her focus to the scene before her and held back an unexpected shudder, not from shame of the family who lived there, but in sympathy for their misfortune. One of the panes on the small front window was broken, a cloth secured over to keep out the cold. Two boards crossed over a section of the roof, no doubt to cover a hole beneath. The corral fence had fallen in a few places; a small hay supply had been left outside to suffer the elements. Nothing indicated anyone lived here, though Amanda thought she heard a cow in the ramshackle structure that likely served as a shelter for livestock. "Have you been here before?"

Colton studied the scene, as surprised as she at what he saw. "Not for a few years when there was a cave-in at the mine. Some of the men from the ranch ride through here from time to time on the way to the mining camp or to hunt in the valley beyond the second ridge, but not since the Beckerts moved in. I recall they were a small family—a husband and wife and their young son." He stopped the horses a short distance from the house. "Wait here until I can check this out."

Amanda assured him she would be fine, but at the imploring look he sent her way, she opted not to argue. She watched as he looked around each side of the small structure before walking to the front door. After a few seconds, a young child appeared in the doorway. Colton spoke with the boy for a minute before returning to the wagon. He helped her down and said, "It's them."

Colton glanced over his shoulder at the boy and again scanned the homestead. "The boy said his father isn't here, and his ma is sleeping."

"What do you mean the father isn't here? If his father left, how have they been surviving way out here?"

Colton shrugged. "That's a good question. Let's go see if we can find out." He held onto her arm in a gentle, but secure grip, and walked beside her to the cabin. "Miss Warren, this young man is Cord Beckert."

Before Amanda could respond, Cord said, "Ma says not to let strangers in the house."

"It's very nice to meet you, Cord. Your mother is a smart person." Amanda peered into the cabin. The fire had gone out, leaving only a few orange embers in the hearth. "Perhaps we can talk for just a few minutes, if that's all right with you."

The boy offered little more than a blank stare. "Do you have any brothers and sisters?"

Cord turned and peeked over his shoulder the cabin's interior. "I had a sister who died of the grippe when she was little."

Amanda glanced askance at Colton before stooping to the boy's eye level. "I lost a sister once, when we were both quite young to the fever. I still miss her very much."

Cord tilted his head and peered at Amanda with sharp gray eyes. "Maybe my sister and yours play together in heaven. That's where Ma said my sister went," the boy added.

"How wonderful that would be." Amanda rose and received a nod of approval and admiration from Colton. She said to Cord, "I know your mother is resting, but you see, we also came out here to invite you both to the town's holiday celebration on Christmas Eve. Would you like to come?"

Cord shrugged. "Pa's got the wagon and horse. Maybe we could come, but I have to ask Ma. We got the mule and he's right good at people riding him."

Colton leaned forward, his eyes steady on the boy's. "I'll come and pick you and your ma up and drive you into town on Christmas Eve, if that's all right. It sure would be a shame to miss the town's Christmas party."

The boy nodded, and then Amanda pulled Colton out of hearing range of the boy. "Would you mind bringing the last basket from the back of the wagon?"

When Colton returned, Amanda thanked him and then handed the basket to Cord. "This is for you and your mother."

"Ma says we can't take no charity."

"It's not charity, it's a gift. Our Christmas gift to you." Amanda held the basket out until Cord accepted it. "Mr. Dawson will return on Christmas Eve just as he promised."

She glanced at Colton. "About noon?" Colton nodded and she continued, "At noon to pick you both up."

Cord remained in the doorway of the cabin until Colton turned the wagon around and drove back to Briarwood. They had driven half an hour before Colton's voice broke through her thoughts.

"It never gets easier, seeing children go without."

"Is that why you do this?"

Colton almost dismissed the question, but then said, "It's not always me. Usually one of the family comes along. We take turns making the rounds of the homesteads a few times per year. Ben and Gabriel went out a few months back." He looked to her. "Maybe you'd like to join Ben next time. Catie may enjoy visiting some of the families, too."

Amanda thought of young Cord. "I do believe Catie would enjoy meeting them. Thank you for having me along today."

"I'm glad for the company."

"I've seen worse, Colton."

Colton glanced at her. "I spent five years in these mountains, and I've seen families with little more than a roof over their head and children with faces so dirty you wonder how their folks tell them apart. Some of those families choose to live that way, but Cord, he didn't look like a happy kid."

Amanda turned her head to study Colton's profile. His jaw was tight and his eyes unreadable. "Where I used to live, there was always a child in need, without a home, family, or a warm fire for the winter. It's difficult any time of the year, but especially at Christmas."

He turned and looked her way. "You have a fine way of looking at things, Miss Amanda. Let's make sure Cord Beckert has a nice Christmas this year."

"Do you think they'll come?"

"I don't know, but I'll be there on Christmas Eve day to pick them up either way."

16

Catie and Brenna sat together on a rug in front of an old trunk that had been stored away in the Gallaghers' attic. When Brenna brought up Catie's idea for the tree decorations, Eliza mentioned the trunk. It had been Victoria Gallagher's treasure chest or so that's what Victoria had told her children. Eliza told them her mother used to bring the trunk out at every Christmas, though her voice had grown quiet when she recounted the memory. Brenna didn't press and made a mental note to ask Ethan about it later.

Eliza was called away by Colton who had a question about one of the young horses they hoped would become part of Hawk's Peak's new breeding program. Brenna swore she watched relief cross over Eliza's features before she left them alone to go through the trunk without her. Brenna recalled the difficulty she experienced after her own father's passing. It had been the first time since her mother's death when she went through her parent's belongings, and the sadness had been overwhelming in the beginning.

Brenna lovingly removed one item at a time as she and Catie admired the care with which the former Mrs. Gallagher had taken with such precious memories. Three small dolls were tucked with care into a blanket. One was homemade and the others reminiscent of the catalog dolls her own mother used to give Brenna as a young girl. A wooden train, perhaps even carved by Ethan's father, rested near the bottom, though the caboose was missing.

Catie held one of the bisque dolls, a beautiful porcelain representation of a young girl with Eliza's dark hair and Gallagher-blue eyes. The striped dress was faded, and the finely stitched hat torn at the edge, but otherwise not a mark marred the porcelain. Catie touched the nose of the doll with a fingertip and followed the smooth lines of the face over the chin and back up to the eyes. The doll was a work of art to be admired, and yet Catie wondered if Eliza ever played with it. She gently lay the doll on the rug beside her and returned to examine the other items with Brenna.

"Will you put some of these on the town tree?" Catie held up a miniature hand-carved rocking horse, a replica of the larger one in Jacob's nursery.

"Why don't we place a few to the side and then we'll let the whole family decide which ones should go on the tree? That rocking horse would make a nice addition, don't you think?"

Catie's head bobbed and her smile tucked up at the edges.

"You're quite taken with horses."

Catie shrugged. "Is that good?"

"Of course. My parents gave me a lovely horse when I was younger than you. Her name is Heather."

"Where is she?"

Brenna smoothed out her bunched skirt and pulled a woven blanket from the trunk. "Oh, she's at my other home in Scotland. A wonderful couple who helped take care of me are looking after her now."

Catie reached out to touch the soft blanket. "Where's Scotland?"

"Far away from here, I'm afraid. It's another country across the Atlantic Ocean." Brenna rested her hands on the edge of the trunk. "Miles and miles of rolling hills surround Cameron Manor. There's a lake nearby where my father used to take me fishing. Even though I didn't like to fish, I enjoyed the stories he would tell me about wild Highlanders and forest fairies. My horse is named for the beautiful flower, which grows on the hill and mountainsides, covering the ground in glorious purple hues." Brenna's mind wandered across the land and sea to her native Scotland.

"Will you ever go back?"

Brenna nodded. "For only a visit, though. I want Jacob to see his mother's land someday, and I do miss it very much. But this is my home, too." She watched the array of emotions flash through Catie's eyes as the child tried to understand, but what child could comprehend two grand homes when they barely knew one?

"Catie, there is something else I need to tell you."

The young girl's light, brown eyes turned to Brenna.

"It's about your birthday."

Catie had always thought of herself as grown up, but now she was thirteen years old, not fourteen. Did one year more of life make a difference? She didn't feel younger. Perhaps it was God's way of giving her more time in a life when there'd been so many difficult years. Catie had spent another blissful day with the Gallaghers, and now she wanted a hundred more.

On this new day, a part of her wanted to go riding again with Eliza, but after she and Brenna picked out some items from the trunk to share with the family, Elizabeth and Amanda asked her to help them in the kitchen. Catie could hunt for supper, but she'd never done much more than heat a little meat or eggs over the fire. When she managed to find a few vegetables, she ate them raw like the wild berries she gathered during the warmer season. Her cooking never smelled that good, either.

They put her to work helping Amanda with a spice cake, and before today, Catie didn't know what a spice cake was, but it tasted delicious. Ethan, Ramsey, and Gabriel had missed dinner, so their absence allowed Catie more time to spend with the ladies. She'd only known the company of her father for most of her life, and it sure was different to be surrounded by womenfolk. She loved their smiles and easy laughter, their kindness that came naturally, and the way they looked after each other and their children. It was a house and family filled with love.

Catie had volunteered to clean up after the meal. Isabelle offered to help so Elizabeth wouldn't feel obliged to stay, and Amanda was told to turn in early, though it took a good deal of prodding to get either woman to leave the kitchen. As they finished cleaning, Catie asked Isabelle what a word meant from *Black Beauty*.

Instead of answering, Isabelle led her into the study and pulled down a leather-bound volume. "This is a dictionary. Many words that you see in books are written down with their meanings."

Catie stared in awe at the thick book. "I can open that book and see what any word means?"

Isabelle opened to a page in the middle. "Most words, yes. Which word do you want to look up first?"

It took Catie a few tries to say the word correctly; it kept coming out as "hustler."

"If you're reading *Black Beauty*, I believe you mean 'hostler.'" Isabelle motioned for Catie to sit in the chair at the desk, and then set the book in front of her. "The words are grouped together by the letters in the alphabet, beginning with A and ending with Z."

Confused and fascinated, Catie ran a finger over the neat

columns of words and definitions.

"How did you teach yourself to read, Catie?"

"My pa taught me the letters, and I learned to put them together."

"That's more than most people manage on their own." Isabelle turned the pages until she reached the section on the letter H. "Begin here and look through the words until you find the one with the same spelling—that looks the same—as the word from the book."

Catie studied each line carefully, discovering a host of words she never realized existed. She stopped her finger next to the word she wanted. "'The person who has the care of horses at the inn.'" She beamed at Isabelle, excited that she'd discovered the meaning, and said, "I would like a job like that."

"I'll leave this book out and ask no one to put it away for a while. Whenever you have a question about a word, you can look it up."

Catie turned her brown eyes up to Isabelle. "Did you used to be the schoolteacher and teach lots of kids?"

"I still am the schoolteacher, for now."

"You don't want to be the teacher anymore?"

Isabelle smiled and smoothed a hand over Catie's braid. "I love teaching, but there's also a time for change."

"Do you think maybe I'll go to school some day?"

Isabelle knelt beside the chair. "Of course, and until we find a new teacher, you can take your lessons here with me in this room. You'll learn more than just what's in books. Eliza will teach you about horses. Brenna can teach you about Scotland and share the stories and lessons she learned from her own father who traveled the world. Ethan and Gabriel will teach you about ranching, and Ramsey can share stories from his own adventures around the country."

"They know so much, don't they?"

Isabelle smiled and brushed a stray hair from Catie's forehead. "Our greatest knowledge doesn't come solely from books but from experiencing life. What would you like to do with an education, Catie?"

When Catie shied away from the question, Isabelle gently placed a hand on the girl's knee and coaxed her to answer. "You can be anyone or anything you want. What have you dreamed about doing some day?"

Catie hesitated for a few seconds, and then said, "I want to do what Eliza does with horses. Can I learn about that at school?"

"School isn't about learning only one subject or one set of ideas. An education gives us a foundation for everything else in life. If you go to school, you'll learn about mathematics, geography, and history."

"What's geography?"

Isabelle rose and tapped the dictionary. Taking her cue, Catie smiled and mentally worked through her letters and then turned the pages back to the letter G and scrolled through the words, sounding out each letter, until she found the word she sought. "A description of the earth."

"That's right."

"Brenna said she's from Scotland and it's far away."

"It is, but when you learn about geography, you study where towns, cities, and countries are on maps. The world is vast with many interesting places to explore and discover."

"Are you from a faraway place?"

Isabelle laughed and sat in one of the chairs opposite the desk. "Not as far away as Scotland. Andrew and I moved here from a place called New Orleans. It's in another part of the country in the state of Louisiana."

Catie twisted and turned, looking around the room. Her eyes settled on the far wall. "I know that's a map, but of where?"

Isabelle rose and motioned Catie to follow. "This is a map of the Montana territory." She indicated a point on the map. "And this is where we are."

Catie stared in awe at the small dot of earth where they stood compared to the grandness of Montana. "Ca—may I stay down here a little longer?"

"Of course. Be sure to blow out the candle and lamp when you go to bed."

Catie nodded and waited until Isabelle left the room. The house creaked and moaned around her but not like the drafty and scary creaks of the little cabin she had shared with her pa. She carried the dictionary to one of the chairs in front of the fire and started reading at the letter A.

Catie looked up when a cool breeze swept through the room and caused the flames to dance. She looked around, but the windows were closed. She returned to section A and the word "abatable," then skipped ahead to section C. She scrolled down, sounding out the word in her head, and stopped at "Christmas." A loud groan brought her head up, and the book slipped from her lap. A fleeting shadow passed by the lamp on the desk, extinguishing the light, and a thin stream of smoke rose through the glass chimney. Catie leaned over to pick up the book and moved closer to the warm hearth, allowing its light to cast a glow around her.

She made a mental note to look up a word for what she was feeling right now. She breathed deeply. "Stay calm, Catie. A big, quiet house makes strange noises." Catie debated blowing out the last lit lamp and heading upstairs to bed, but she was saved from having to walk up there alone. Isabelle's hurried steps brought her back into the study.

"I was in the kitchen enjoying a cup of tea, but then I heard the loud thud and though you might have hurt yourself."

Catie stared wide-eyed at Isabelle. "I didn't hear a thud." She motioned Isabelle closer and lowered her voice to a whisper. "I think you have a ghost." Catie expected to be mocked or told it was only her imagination, but Isabelle did neither. Instead, she took the dictionary from Catie, deposited it on the desk, and picked up the candle.

"It's time for bed now. You go along and wait for me in the hall."

Once the young girl left the room, Isabelle made a slow circle, peering into every shadow. By the fire's warmth, she listened to the house moan and sign on a cold, dark night, but nothing else appeared or made its presence known.

"I'm telling you, Hawk's Peak is haunted." Isabelle placed a napkin on Andrew's lap and set a bowl of hot oats in front of him. "I'm telling you, I sensed something in the study last night. I experienced the same sensation the time when our old housekeeper in New Orleans told me about a ghost that haunted the park near our home. It was said a pair of lovers were found near the walking path late one night by the girl's father."

Isabelle glanced around at her rapt audience and continued. "In a rage, the father took his daughter away, but the young man refused to part from her. The following night, the girl sneaked from her home and met the young man in the park. They were found the next morning in the river. The housekeeper said the couple have haunted the park ever since."

Amanda chuckled, Catie kept her head low and focused on her breakfast, and Elizabeth raised a brow.

"Did you ever see the ghosts, Ibby?"

Isabelle rested her hands in her lap and sighed. "No, I did not, but that doesn't mean they weren't there."

Brenna, who smiled softly, appeared to be the only one more interested in the ghosts than in teasing her sister-in-law. "Cameron Manor is haunted."

All eyes turned to Brenna. Andrew giggled and asked, "There are lots of ghosts! Can we see the ghost here?"

Catie spoke up. "You can't see ghosts, Andrew."

Brenna bounced Jacob on her lap and said, "I don't know about that. I once saw the lady who haunted Cameron Manor. Night was coming, and that's when she came out, between the moment of day and darkness. She floated past a window on the second-story balcony where I was playing. Her long gray dress billowed in the wind, and her hair, like the color of spun gold, trailed down her back in long curls. I didn't see her face, though."

Catie waited for fear to take root, but she wasn't frightened. "Did the ghost scare you?"

Brenna looked away as though remembering a time gone past. "Not at all. I recall a peaceful feeling, after the initial surprise. I told Iain—the man who looks after the house—about it once. He said, the Lady of the Manor—that's what they called her— had visited them every Christmas Eve for as long as he could remember. He said he'd been there long enough so he knew when to expect her. However, it was best to leave her alone."

"Maybe we do have a Christmas ghost," Andrew chimed in.

"A ghost where?" Ethan sauntered into the kitchen, red-faced beneath his dark beard. He was by his wife's chair in three strides and bent to kiss her lips and the top of Jacob's head.

"Isabelle believes Hawk's Peak is haunted," Brenna said.

Ethan pressed his lips together to prevent the laughter from escaping. "I've lived here most of my life, and I've never seen a ghost."

"Brenna said she saw a Christmas ghost before." Catie looked expectantly between Brenna and Ethan.

"Well, if the ranch is haunted, then I have no intention of riling up our visitors." Ethan ate a slice of bacon off his wife's plate before Elizabeth slapped his hand away and set a fresh plate of food in front of him. Ethan walked to the washbasin to clean his hands and then returned to the table. To Isabelle he said, "Gabriel rode back with me, should be in shortly."

"How . . ." Isabelle glanced at the back of Catie's head. "Are things in town?"

Ethan chose his words carefully. "Not as I had hoped they'd be on some accounts, but the townsfolk sure are looking forward to this Christmas party. The reverend has even gathered a small group together to sing carols on Christmas Eve."

"I haven't done that in ages." Brenna handed Jacob to Amanda who had asked for a little baby time with him, and then refilled Ethan's coffee. "Catie had a grand idea of her own. We spent yesterday going through one of your mother's old trunks."

Ethan smiled. "Her treasure chest. I haven't thought about that in years." He turned to Catie. "Tell me about this idea of yours."

"We're going to hang treasures on the town tree. Brenna said we—the family—could choose which treasures together."

Ethan squeezed Catie's shoulder and met his wife's gaze over Catie's head, but said to the young girl, "Then you should be the first one to choose."

When breakfast ended, Ethan managed to entice Brenna back upstairs. He'd been apart from her too long of late, and he missed holding her. They lay together on the bed, a quilt drawn up over Brenna. Ethan's arm circled her waist, his hand resting on her stomach. The movement surprised him as much as Brenna.

Ethan leaned forward. "Was that—"

"The baby." Brenna's grin brightened any dark clouds of weariness that had settled over Ethan the past few days. "It's the first time I've felt him move."

Ethan waited for another kick, but the baby had apparently decided it was time to rest. "I'm sorry I wasn't there for you and

Jacob in the beginning." Ethan remembered the long journey he took to Scotland to win Brenna back and bring her home. He was there for Jacob's birth, but he'd missed so much before his son was born.

Brenna cupped her husband's face, her adoring eyes mirroring the love in his. "You were there from the beginning. From the moment it all mattered, you were there. And now you'll have another chance to experience it all again."

"And I'm going to enjoy every minute."

Brenna's smile turned playful. "Even when I'm at my grumpiest? Iain said I behaved like a wild Highlander during my first few months back in Scotland."

Ethan returned the lighthearted grin. "I think it was because you missed me. I know I missed you." He sobered unexpectedly.

"What's wrong, Ethan?"

He gazed upon his wife and pressed a hand to her middle. "I can't imagine a father who would do what Joseph Carr has done to Catie. He left her with nothing, and now he's going to prison for a long time."

Brenna's hand halted caressing Ethan's arm. "What do you mean?"

"I didn't want Catie to know, at least until I figured out how to tell her. Joseph helped his brother rob the train outside of Bozeman a few months back. That's why Cyrus came after Catie; he wanted the money he'd given to Joseph for safekeeping."

"Does he still have the money?"

Ethan nodded. "That's why Gabe and I took so long to get back this morning."

"Did you find it?"

Ethan's hand moved up his wife's arm, and he massaged the back of her neck. "Right where he said it would be. I don't know if Joseph's conscience got the better of him or if he planned to keep the money. In the end, it will mean something to Catie that he told the truth. I'll take the money back to the bank with a few of the men in case there's any trouble."

"Are you expecting any?"

"No. Cyrus is halfway to Bozeman by now with the deputies, but I'd rather not take unnecessary risk." Ethan bent his head forward and brushed his lips over Brenna's. "I have too much to live for these days."

Brenna returned the kiss and sank against his chest. "Yes, you do. We're truly blessed. We have family who would do anything for each other, a healthy son, and another one the way."

"I'm hoping for a daughter who looks like her mother."

Brenna's smile widened as she played with the buttons on Ethan's shirt. "She might get my temper, too."

"Then it's a good thing I have experience with feisty Highlanders."

She lightly pinched his side. "Have you now?" They relaxed into a comfortable silence and rested for a few minutes, mulling in their own thoughts. "Ethan? What's going to happen with Catie now that her father is going to prison?" Brenna leaned up on an elbow and looked down at her husband. His beautiful blue eyes were hidden beneath lids heavy with exhaustion. Had she not known him better, she might have thought he'd fallen asleep.

"Joseph doesn't want his daughter going to an orphanage." When Ethan said nothing else, Brenna nudged him. He opened his eyes and sat up, bracing his back against the headboard. "He wants us—the family—to adopt Catie."

Brenna's heart fluttered and she fought to curb the tears of relief threatening to spill. "Truly?"

"We have to put the question to Catie."

"Yes, she told us she wants to stay."

Ethan held his wife's face in his hands. "I know. I've been thinking about what's best for Catie, and where she might want to live. She and Eliza are so alike, and Catie loves spending time with Andrew."

"Why does it have to be a choice?" Brenna pressed her lips to his and grinned. "She has a family here—all of us—and no matter which roof she lives under, this ranch is her home." Brenna leaned back and looked around the room. "You told me once this place, this home, has been the foundation of Hawk's Peak from the beginning. It seems fitting that Catie should make her new beginning here, as so many of us have."

"You amaze me." Ethan pulled her close and kissed her brow. "Every day, you amaze me." He sobered. "There's something else. Joseph wants to see Catie."

Brenna released the breath she'd been holding. "I believe Catie may wish to see him, if only to say goodbye. Joseph Carr made some mistakes, and I can't forgive a father for leaving a child the way he did, but that doesn't make him an evil man."

"We'll tell Catie today. I don't know how long her father will be in the Briarwood jail. Ramsey sent a telegram to the judge."

"She's stronger than any of us realize." Brenna scooted off the bed and brushed her skirts down. "Catie's with Jacob. We should tell her now and give her time to think things over before she goes into town."

"You're sure she'll go?"

Brenna held out her hand to Ethan. "I would. Don't you remember a stubborn Scottish woman who came here looking for the grandfather who abandoned his family? I knew then that he wasn't a good man, but I needed to see for myself. At least Catie will know her father loves her, no matter what." They started for the door, but Brenna stopped, forcing Ethan to step back.

"What's wrong?"

She drew his hand back to her stomach. "He's moving again."

"She?"

"Or he," She smiled. "It will be Isabelle's turn soon."

Ethan stepped around his wife and held her still. "You know?"

Brenna laughed, a rich, bright laughter that temporarily drove away the vestiges of gloom hovering over their impending task. "Of course I know. We all do. We only pretend not to know until Isabelle and Gabriel give us the good news."

Ethan grinned and draped an arm around his wife's shoulders. "Well, at least I can tell Gabriel I kept my promise."

The revelry died down when they came together in the study with Catie where she'd been reading to Jacob. Enthralled with her voice, Jacob was focused more on her than on the wooden blocks in front of him. Andrew had sat down to enjoy the story, and it took some coaxing and a bribe of cookies for him to take his puppy into the kitchen.

Catie remained silent throughout Ethan's explanation of what happened to her father, though he surprised himself and Brenna when he left out the details of what Joseph had done. "He'd like to see you, but it's your decision. If you want to see him, I'll drive you into town today."

Catie twisted the edge of her skirt. "I should talk to my pa. He tried, but I guess we all make mistakes, huh?"

"I guess we do." Ethan stared in awe and with pride at the young girl who was wise beyond her years. "Bundle up and we'll leave as soon as the wagon is ready."

Brenna held out her hand to Catie who stood while Ethan lifted Jacob into his arms. "Let's go and get you ready to see your father."

Nerves and the new coat Brenna bought her kept Catie warm on the long drive to town. When they arrived, Ethan drove to the general store rather than the jail. He helped Brenna down first and then Catie before escorting them both inside.

"Loren." Ethan tipped the edge of his hat to the storekeeper.

"Good to see you, Ethan, Brenna. My Joanna has talked of nothing but this party for days." Loren came around the counter.

"And, you've brought me a visitor."

Ethan placed a hand on Catie's shoulder, calming her. "I did, though I believe you've met."

Loren held out his hand for Catie to shake. His friendly smile and kind eyes helped to ease the remainder of her nerves.

"It's a real pleasure to see you again, Catie." Loren straightened and tapped the side of his forehead. "Now, if memory serves, you're partial to the books. Why don't you pick out a piece of candy and we'll have a look at a couple of new books that have arrived."

Catie looked up at Brenna. "Can—may I?"

"You go ahead. I'll be back for you both in a few minutes."

Catie now knew when Ethan left and said he'd return, he meant it. Brenna was drawn away by the storekeeper's wife, and grateful she had a few minutes longer before she saw her pa, she pointed to the licorice and enjoyed a piece while Mr. Baker showed her the books. Her eyes immediately went to a new copy of *Little Women.*

"Ah, you've found one you like, then." Loren pulled the thick volume from the shelf. "It's one of my dear wife's favorites."

Catie smoothed her hand over the hard cover in reverence. "How much does it cost?"

"Well, now that one isn't for sale, only for trade."

Catie started to put the book back on the shelf and then pulled it back down. "What kind of trade?"

"These windows could use a washing on the inside, and I'll have a few small deliveries here in town I could use some help with. It's busy around the holidays. What do you say, Miss Catie?"

"And then I get to keep the book?"

Loren chuckled. "That's how it works."

Catie grinned up at him. "It's a deal, Mr. Baker." This time she held out her hand to shake and then replaced the book. He took it right back off the shelf.

"You hold onto this. No sense in a good book going unread."

Her grin widened. "When can I start?"

The metal chest filled with the mining company's payroll was now stored in the bank's safe. Ethan's long strides would have covered the distance between the jail and general store in less than a minute had he not been waylaid by the blacksmith, Otis, about how to fancy up—Otis's words—the sleigh for the Christmas party. Ethan had no idea what Otis was talking about, but he replied with, "Ribbon and pine, I guess."

Otis bobbed his head and hurried back to his shop. Then Tilly caught him outside of her café and asked if he preferred apple or pecan pie. Not having a preference for one over the other, he replied with, "Apple pecan."

She nodded and went back into her café. Ethan almost made it to the store when young Foster stepped out of the telegraph office and asked him if he could bring his dog to the party. "Of course you can," Ethan had replied, and hoped the dog was trained well enough not to eat any of Tilly's apple pecan pies off the table.

The reverend opened the general store door as Ethan reached for the handle. "Ethan, I'm glad you're here." Reverend Philips clapped his hands together and folded them beneath his smile. "I could use your advice about the nativity."

Ethan let the door close. "Nativity?"

"Yes, I thought a nativity would be just the thing."

"Well, it's a good idea, Reverend."

"Oh, wonderful!" Reverend Philips waved his hands in an animated gesture Ethan never quite understood. "We'll build it in the back of the church, too cold outside, of course. What about sheep?"

"Sheep, Reverend?"

"Yes, sheep for the nativity."

Ethan held back his laughter because he saw the reverend was serious. "We should probably not have the sheep inside the church, but the rest of it sounds good."

"Of course, of course. We'll save the sheep for another time." Reverend Philips patted Ethan on the shoulder and said as he walked away, "Otis is just the man to help build the nativity, don't you think?"

Ethan didn't bother to answer since the reverend hadn't stopped long enough to wait for one. He entered the store and saw Brenna ensconced with Joanna Baker in the fabric section. He found Catie reading on a stool behind the counter. She jumped down when she saw him and held up the book for her to see.

"Mr. Baker said I could trade for the book." She missed the wink Loren sent Ethan. "I just have to wash the windows and make deliveries."

"Sounds like you're a smart businessperson. What's the book?"

Catie held it up. "*Little Women.* It's my favorite. Have you read it?"

"Nope, but Brenna has, and I imagine the rest of the women at the ranch. You could form some kind of reading club and talk about it. That's a good trade." Ethan helped Catie back into her coat. "Are you ready for our next stop?"

Catie hugged the book close. "I'm ready."

Brenna said goodbye to Joanna, and they all started for the door when Loren called out.

"Oh, Ethan. I have a question about the Christmas party."

By the time they managed to leave the store—Loren pulled

Ethan aside and wanted to know if someone was chosen to dress up as Santa Claus, because if not, he had a brother visiting who wanted the part—Ethan was half an hour past the time he told Ramsey they'd be there. The bell above the jailhouse door rang when they entered, but a signal to their arrival wasn't necessary. Ramsey stood between the door and the woodstove where Joseph Carr sat drinking coffee. When Catie spotted her father, the hold on her new book tightened.

Joseph stood, his hands free of iron. Ethan removed his hat and glanced at Ramsey before guiding Catie the rest of the way inside. He planned to help ease the tension, but Brenna was right—Catie was stronger than any of them realized. She crossed the room to stand in front of her father while Ethan and Brenna stood close behind her.

"Did you do a bad thing, Pa?"

Joseph lowered himself back into the chair. "Yes, I did, Catherine Rose, and I'm sorry for it, but I'm most sorry that I left you alone."

"You're going away again, aren't you?"

Joseph nodded. "For a long while, but not because I want to."

"Because you did something bad?"

"Yes."

Catie rummaged in the pocket of her dress and held out a silver locket. "You should maybe keep this to remember me and Ma by."

Ethan swore he saw Joseph's eyes glisten.

"I'll keep you right here." Joseph pressed a fist to his heart. "Your ma would've wanted you to have this." He helped her put the locket around her neck. "You'll be good and listen to the Gallaghers, won't you?"

Catie looked over her shoulder at Ethan and Brenna. "I get to stay with you?"

Ethan nodded. "If that's what you want."

With a solemn smile, Catie turned back to her father. "I'll be good, Pa, I promise."

"That's my girl. Now, why don't you show me what you've got there?"

17

Ramsey had convinced the marshal that Joseph couldn't get a fair trial in the same town where his brother would be tried and sentenced. The marshal service agreed to take him to Deer Lodge instead.

Catie had insisted on standing there as her father was escorted away, for support, she had told them. Brenna stood close to the girl on the right while Ethan and Ramsey stood on her left.

When Joseph and the marshal had ridden out of sight, Brenna said, "I smelled something wonderful baking when we passed Tilly's. Why don't we go and see what she's cooked up."

Though reluctant to leave the spot where she watched her pa taken away, Catie stepped in beside Brenna and Eliza. Ramsey excused himself, but promised he wouldn't be long.

Brenna's heart ached to see a strong and vivacious child sink into her own despair, but she knew from personal experience that pushing her would only drive Catie deeper. She needed time to deal with the loss of her father and knowing the truth about what he'd done. While Catie sat quietly, they engaged Tilly in conversation, and then the telegraph operator's wife when she came into the café. A few of Tilly's patrons stopped at the table to say hello or express their excitement about Christmas Eve.

Once they'd concluded lunch, they continued back to the

general store so Brenna could pick up the fabrics Joanna promised to hold for her.

"Ethan, Brenna," Ben said, tipping the edge of his hat. "Miss Catie."

Ethan looked at the supplies stacked on the counter. "We could have picked these up." He took a closer look at the items. "Did Elizabeth send you back into town?"

"I volunteered." Ben motioned Ethan aside when Brenna and Catie walked to the fabric section. "One of the men from the mining camp happened upon Colton while he was out hunting. It seems someone up that way mentioned Hawk's Peak and Joseph Carr. The miner didn't know what it meant, but he was on his way to town and thought he'd better say something. Seeing Colton out there saved him a ride to the ranch."

Ethan considered, and then thought of the silent partner Joseph mentioned Cyrus had. "Did the miner say anything else?"

Ben shook his head. "Colton said he wanted to stay at the ranch and scout the area. I have the other men rotating shifts, so everything is covered. I figured I'd come into town and send a telegram while I was here." Ben nodded toward Catie. "I didn't think you'd want to be apart from her today, considering."

"I don't, and I appreciate it, Ben. I know we've burdened you with more than usual lately."

"It's not a burden. Besides, Elizabeth has promised some of our favorite desserts this year, and to my way of thinking, that's all the thanks we need." He grinned, lightening the mood.

Ethan smiled. "I'll speak with Colton once we get back to the ranch." He examined the stack of goods when they returned to the counter. "What exactly are they baking?"

"I didn't ask, but this Christmas party has everyone excited. Everywhere I've been today, folks have been talking about it." Ben added a few more items to the stack on the counter while Loren went into the back room. "Loren said business has never been so good; women buying new material for dresses and for new shirts for the men."

Loren strode back in carrying a sack of sugar, which Ben lifted from his arms and set on the counter. Loren sighed and told him, "Sold out of red ribbon yesterday and candles the day before. Had to order more." Loren peered at Ethan over his narrow-rimmed spectacles. "This is some idea, Ethan."

"It's wonderful to know the townspeople are looking forward to this event so much, but it wasn't my idea. You have the women of Hawk's Peak to thank for that."

Loren wiggled a finger and said, "I've thanked your wife, and Joanna will thank her again a few times before you leave here." To Ben he asked, "Anything else for you today?"

Ben nodded. "With all the extra baking they have planned, Amanda and Elizabeth wanted to be sure they didn't run out of supplies."

"Oh, well, you won't. I'm adding an extra bag of pecans and dried cranberries, and some spices that just came in from San Francisco."

Ben laughed. "They'll appreciate it, though I reckon Elizabeth will see through your motives. I believe I've delivered one or two of her spiced apple cranberry cakes to you before."

Loren feigned innocence, inciting laughter from Ethan who hefted one of the two larger crates of items from the counter. "I'll be right back, Brenna," he called out.

Catie remained silent most of the drive back to the ranch. She didn't speak until they spotted three wolves crossing their path one hundred yards ahead of them. "I haven't seen one before."

Ethan handed the reins to Brenna and pulled a rifle from beneath the bench. "They're beautiful and hungry. They're hunting."

"You can't shoot them."

"I don't plan to shoot them, Catie." Ethan checked the bullets, and they waited for the small pack to pass them by. "Have you ever hunted larger game?" When Catie shook her head, he continued, "Wolves, mountain lions, and bears are better hunters than we are. They don't want to tangle with humans any more than we want to with them, but if they get hungry enough, they'll come after whatever they can, including people. Most times, they keep to themselves in the mountains and forests."

"Have they ever attacked you?"

Ethan and Brenna exchanged a glance. Ethan said, "They've come after me before and Eliza once. Most of the ranch hands have come across them at least once."

"But you got away."

Ethan nodded. "That's right."

"Did you kill one before?"

"It's not something any of us like to do, but if there's no other choice—if it's your life or theirs—you save yourself. That's one of the most important rules of hunting. The other is to never kill anything you don't have to."

Ethan watched as the wolves burst across the fields and into the trees. "They must have caught the scent of something else." He handed the rifle to Catie. "Why don't you hold onto that and be our lookout."

Catie accepted the rifle, the familiar weight comfortable in her hands until they reached the ranch. Ramsey and Eliza stood on the porch, wrapped in each other's arms and a couple of warm blankets. Ramsey kissed his wife and then stepped down when the wagon rolled to a stop. "I've been waiting for your return. Ethan and I have been volunteered to cut down a tree for the town."

Amused, Ethan smiled at Eliza. "I suppose we can handle that, but I'm not good at picking out trees. How about you, Ramsey?"

Ramsey sighed and shook his head. "Eliza's the real tree hunter in the family."

Eliza caught on and said, "I admit, I know how to pick out the best tree. Unfortunately, it's my turn to rotate in working the horses. Tell you what, Catie. Why don't you go in my place and pick out a real nice tree for the town, and then you can come back and help brush down and feed the horses."

Catie appeared skeptical, and Eliza shot Brenna a glare because her sister-in-law looked like she was going to start laughing. "Is there such a thing as a Christmas tree hunter, Eliza?"

Eliza held a hand to her heart. "On my honor, that's what Ramsey called me." She didn't mention that today was the first time she'd ever been called a Christmas tree hunter. Eliza preferred the biggest tree she could find, and after two years of picking out the tree in her youth, and then having to keep it outside because it wouldn't fit in the living room, she was relegated to driving the horse and sleigh her father pulled out each year when the snow was too deep to reach the forest with a wagon.

The arrangement suited Eliza perfectly, and so did sending her brother and husband off into the woods with Catie to pick out this year's tree. "While you're out there, you may as well pick one for the house."

"Not necessary," Ethan grinned and pushed back the brim of his hat. "Gabriel and Ben took care of that this morning before Ben went into town." Ethan turned to Catie. "So, what do you say? You want to help us pick out a tree?"

Catie's smile reached her eyes as she nodded in a firm yes.

They paired Catie with the mare she'd ridden the first time out with Ethan. It was like coming together again with an old friend, and the mare seemed as keen with Catie as she with the animal. Ramsey rode alongside her, leading Ethan's stallion, while Ethan drove the team and sleigh. Once they reached the edge of the forest and secured the team, Ethan switched to his stallion and they finished their trek into the deep woods.

Streaks of sunlight broke through the treetops, filtering through snow-covered pine boughs. Catie slid off the mare and secured her horse to a tree like she'd been taught—wrapping the reins around a low branch but not too tight that the horse couldn't get away in an emergency. She patted the mare's neck, and in the tall boots Brenna loaned her, she trudged into the woods. Every pine tree looked alike to her, but Ethan pointed out the difference in some of the needles and cones and that some didn't have cones or needles during the winter. Most of the trees were shaped like an upside down triangle with jagged edges, and it was those she studied, searching for the one that would be the town's Christmas tree. Catie wanted to choose carefully because the townfolks were counting on a special tree.

In the center of a copse of thick trees and fallen logs, a halo of light surrounded a single pine. Catie thought she heard a chorus of song, but she did see a fluttering of birds as the branches sparkled, illuminating the forest until all shreds of darkness disappeared.

"Do you see one you like?"

Catie blinked a few times, but the dimness of the forest had returned and the music she thought she'd heard no longer echoed through the trees. "That one."

Ethan and Ramsey looked where she pointed at a magnificent and enormous tree.

The ride back to the ranch was slowed due to the size of the tree, but Catie's smile was all the reason Ethan needed to haul the giant pine back to the ranch, and later into town. Colton approached them from the east, his white and cinnamon-colored horse prancing in the snow. "You found the town's tree."

Ethan nodded to Catie. "Our new tree hunter did."

"Eliza will be disappointed to learn she's been dethroned." Colton winked, bringing a grin to Catie's lips.

Colton looked to Ramsey, held his gaze for just a moment, and then waited for him to occupy Catie by telling her about the mountain range to the west. Colton leaned forward and lowered his voice as he continued to ride alongside the sleigh while Ethan drove. "I believe I've found Cyrus's partner."

Ethan made sure Catie was still speaking with Ramsey before replying. "Where?"

"One set of tracks have crisscrossed over the area around the trappers' cabin, and it looks as though someone has been staying there since the payroll was recovered. Those same tracks made a path from Ramsey's place to the main house and then moved along the forest edge."

"Like the person was scouting?"

"Could be. Those same tracks moved north. I followed them a few miles, and they never backtracked. I can't guarantee without following whoever it is all the way, but I'd wager the person is on their way to Desperate Creek. My guess is that when he didn't find the money, he moved on."

Ethan's shoulders relaxed, the tension he'd been holding in seeped from his body. He had worried that with the possibility of Cyrus's partner on the loose, Catie wouldn't be safe after all.

Colton was quick to add, "He could still come back around, but we'll keep a close watch on the area for a while. From the tracks, I'd say he's not a big man."

Ethan and Colton both turned at the sound of Catie's young laughter filling a void of silence around them. At least for now, Catie was safe, and they'd keep her that way.

18

"You found quite a tree, Ethan." Reverend Philips paced in front of the giant pine and then disappeared around the back before reappearing on the other side. "Quite a tree, indeed."

"Catie chose it." Ethan was quick to clarify, but the humor in his eyes said he enjoyed the idea of people's reaction. "We told her she could pick any tree she wanted."

Ramsey and Gabriel finished securing the tree in the large wooden stand they'd had to build around the trunk.

"And she picked the best and biggest they could carry." Gabriel had laughed when he first saw the tree hanging over the back of the wagon, and then asked who the unlucky people were who would haul the tree into town. He should have kept quiet.

Gabriel and Ramsey fell into line beside Ethan and Catie to admire their work. The blue spruce stood nearly twenty feet tall with full branches ready to hold an array of ribbons, candles, and whatever decorations the townsfolk brought with them.

"When do we get to decorate it?" she asked.

"In a few days on Christmas Eve," Ramsey replied. His gaze raised to the sky. "Let's hope it doesn't snow."

Reverend Philips circled the tree once more and then joined them. A small crowd had gathered nearby, pointing and whispering about the tree. Catie couldn't hear what they said, but every person she noticed wore a smile. She leaned back and tilted her head, bumping against Ethan's chest. "Do we have to wait for Christmas Eve?"

"Pretty sight, isn't it?"

Amanda smiled at Colton when he approached from the general store, his arms holding a wooden crate filled with what appeared to be nails and small tools. "Beautiful. I rode into town with them just to see it standing for the first time. I haven't seen a tree so grand in the middle of town before." Amanda peeked around him at the house down the road. "What are you and Ben doing over there?"

Colton tipped back his hat. "A Christmas project."

Amanda watched Ben heave a stack of heavy boards from the back of a wagon. "Whose house is that?"

"It will be the Beckert's when we finish."

Surprised, Amanda turned to the ranch hand. "I don't understand. They bought the house?"

"It's rented to them for now. We figure Cord should spend Christmas in their new home."

"One might begin to think that Hawk's Peak is a gathering place for saints and angels." At Colton's confused look, Amanda explained, "From what I've learned in my time there, everyone except Ethan, Gabriel, and Eliza were either searching, running, or had nowhere else to go until they reached Hawk's Peak. I imagine many of you have stories you've never shared, but in the end, you also found a home there."

The crowd dispersed as the townspeople went about their day. A few remained behind to admire the tree and to congratulate Catie on a remarkable job well done. Amanda turned and faced Colton. "Would you mind if I walked with you?"

Colton stepped aside. "Not at all."

They approached the small house. Ben's back was to them as he sawed the end of a board. Despite the frigid air and ice forming on the edges of the roof, Ben worked without his coat. Colton cleared his throat, and when he saw Ben had noticed Amanda, Colton excused himself to go inside.

"This is a wonderful thing you're doing for the Beckerts."

Seemingly uncomfortable with the praise, Ben said, "Colton told me what you two saw when you went out there. Seems the right thing to do."

"The Beckerts are lucky to have you as a champion."

Ben drank long and deep from his canteen. "It could just be that luck has a way of finding people when they need it most."

Amanda didn't miss the flash in Ben's eyes before he looked away, and she regretted it. She knew it was her actions that caused his hesitation around her. Amanda understood some people were not comfortable with admiration for their charitable works, but she had yet to ascertain Ben's reluctance in that regard. She left him to finish the porch, her excuse that she had to get back to the ranch with the others.

When her father, back at the jail, asked if Catie wanted to stay with the Gallaghers, there had been no hesitation in her heart, but her mind still echoed with thoughts of doubt and guilt. Her pa went away again, and this time he wasn't coming back. She was living the life he had tried to give her but failed.

Ramsey and Eliza rode beside her to the top of a crest where they could see the ranch in its entirety. "This is all Hawk's Peak, Catie," Eliza began. "No matter where you go on the land you see, it's home."

Catie gazed at the landscape. From here, the houses still looked grand but small compared to the mountains, which towered in the distance on three sides. "It's bigger than I thought."

Ramsey leaned forward to rub his hand up and down his horse's neck. "It seems that way when you're riding through the snow, but it's not so bad the rest of the year."

Catie smiled up at him. "I like riding in the snow. It sure beats walking in it."

Ramsey chuckled. "Well, you're good at it. Eliza and I will have to watch out for you; one day you'll be able to run a ranch better than we can."

Catie's smile faded and she glanced between the two of them. Eliza took this as her cue to speak. "We wanted you to see the ranch as it is now. This land wasn't always a place of peace, and miles of fences separated one side from the other. It's finally whole, as it should have been all along, and it's your home now, and for as long as you want it to be."

Her breath hitched, and afraid the water in her eyes would spill over into tears, Catie turned her gaze back to the ranch. "I can work hard and earn my keep. I won't let anyone down."

Ramsey leaned forward and rested his arms on the pommel. "We know that, and hard work is a part of ranch life, but you've had to grow up too fast for someone your age. We'll teach you everything you want to know about ranching, but there's a whole world out there, and you'll have the opportunity, if you want, to see more of it."

Catie had spent the following hours, up through dinner, thinking about what Ramsey had said. She remembered the map of Montana Territory that Isabelle had showed her and thought of how small it must really be compared to a whole world. One day, she vowed to see more—perhaps even Brenna's Scotland.

Later in the evening after the family meal ended, Ethan and Brenna asked Catie to join them in the study. Brenna sat in one of the plush chairs by the fire, and Ethan stood beside his wife, offering the empty chair to Catie. The room had become a comfortable and welcoming place for her, easing her nerves, and she sat across from them. "Did I do something wrong?"

Brenna and Ethan both shook their heads, quick to reassure her. Brenna said, "Absolutely not. Why ever would you think so?"

Catie shuffled her feet over the rug. "Pa used to sit me down after supper when I did something wrong."

"You've done nothing wrong," Ethan promised. "What we have to speak with you about is good, or we believe it is."

Brenna leaned forward and held Catie's hands between hers. "We have a letter to a judge—two letters, in fact—and we'd like you to read them before we mail them."

Ethan handed Catie two sheets of paper. Confused, she read the top letter. It wasn't long, just a few sentences, and at the bottom a signature line. "Is that my pa's name?"

Ethan nodded. "It is. Go ahead and read the second letter before we talk."

Catie did as requested. By the time she reached the end, a single teardrop had fallen on the paper. When she looked back up, a glossy sheen had brightened her brown eyes. "I get to live with you? For all time?"

Ethan grinned, even as Brenna released one of her hands from Catie to grip her husband's. "For all time," Brenna said through a few tears of her own. "If that's what you want."

Catie stared agape at them both. Ethan had found her, and Brenna loved her as a mother should. Jacob was the younger brother she'd always wanted, and so was Andrew. Isabelle and Gabriel treated her like a sister—someone to whom they could teach. Gabriel managed to always make her laugh. Catie didn't know what it was like to have a grandmother, but Elizabeth was everything she ever imagined one would be. Amanda was the soft-spoken friend who hid behind secrets, she suspected, but showed tenderness and kindness to others. They would be her family now.

"Will I see my pa again?"

Ethan knelt beside the chair and rested a hand on Catie's arm. "If you'd like to see him again, we'll find a way for you to visit him, but it could be a long time before he's free."

Catie covered Ethan's large, well-worked hand with her small and smooth hand. "You won't ever go away, will you?"

In an instant, Catie was in his arms. "You'd be stuck with us for a very long time."

Brenna's laughter blended with tears, and before Catie realized what she was doing, she moved to Brenna and circled her neck with her arms. "I'd like to be stuck with you for a very, very long time."

When she climbed beneath the covers that night, peace enveloped her and she believed with her whole heart that everything would be all right. When she woke, the sky outside her window was still black and not a star shined. Catie tossed off the covers and crossed the room, pushing aside the heavy drapery to look outside. Snow fell in a quiet curtain, and Catie longed to open the window and allow the fresh winter air inside. Instead, she added another log to the fire that burned low in her room.

A shadow passed behind her, and the flames fluttered, then extinguished. Catie spun and held onto the back of a chair. A soft glow in front of the window began to grow. The faint melody of a woman's song became clearer. Catie feared little, but when the glow filled half the room, she expected her heart to pound through her chest, but instead, a sense of calm washed through her. She didn't recognize the woman, except her eyes reminded her of Ethan and her smile of Gabriel. Her long dark hair flowed straight down her back like Eliza's.

The woman beckoned Catie to come closer. She pointed out the window. Her lips moved, but Catie heard only song, and she didn't recognize the tune. The woman floated closer, tears falling down her pale face even as her smile brightened. She pointed again outside and then looked to the chest of drawers before looking once more out the window.

Catie's eyes opened and her heart did pound within her chest. The fire burned low, just as it had when she fell asleep. Catie was alone in the room, safe and warm beneath the quilts. She pushed aside the blankets and climbed out of bed. She crossed the room to watch the snow fall against the darkness, then turned and studied the room. A few minutes passed as her breathing slowed. Just a dream, she thought. Only a dream. The fire needed another log, and then Catie lit the lamp beside her bed.

The bureau stood against the wall beside the small hearth. Catie hadn't touched anything in the room save to get ready for sleep. She walked to the chest of drawers and opened the top one to find a few linens. The next two drawers were empty, as was the last. She opened the top drawer again and removed the linens. Nothing. When she attempted to close the drawer, it caught and refused to close. Catie jimmied and shifted to pry open the drawer and pull it out. She stumbled back.

"Ouch!" Catie rubbed her shin where the edge of the drawer hit, and then she saw them.

Catie bent down to retrieve a bundle of letters tied with ribbon. Some of the edges were torn from the foray with the stuck drawer. A fine print was scrolled across the front of the top envelope. Jacob Gallagher, it read, with an address in Texas. Where was Texas? She told herself to ask Isabelle in the morning, but she didn't want to wait until morning before telling someone about her discovery. Surely they must know, but if they didn't, wouldn't they want to know? Catie set the bundle on the bureau and returned the drawer and linens to the bureau.

Catie sat on the edge of the trunk and stared at the letters. She wouldn't dare open them but that didn't stop her imagination from concocting her own story about what they might hold.

At the first indication someone else might be awake, Catie sneaked into the hallway, careful not to wake anyone else who preferred to sleep past half past four in the morning. She caught sight of the edge of a white robe flowing behind someone as they entered another room from the hallway. Certain that it wasn't her dream ghost again, Catie tiptoed down to Jacob's nursery. Brenna lifted her son from the crib as Catie walked on stockinged feet into the room.

"Catie, you startled me." Brenna held her son against her shoulder and rubbed his back. "Jacob was fussing, which is why I'm awake, but what are you doing up at this hour?"

"I woke up about an hour ago. Can—may I talk to you and Ethan?" Catie held the bundle of letters in front of her. "I have something to show you."

"Come closer so I can see what you have there." Brenna shifted Jacob to her other hip and peered down at the letters. "Oh my. Wherever did you find those?"

Catie considered for a moment and then said, "I'm not sure you'd believe me, or if it was real."

Someone else might have mocked or showed skepticism, but Brenna said, "You'd be surprised at what I believe." Brenna passed Jacob into Catie's willing arms and accepted the letters in return. She pulled back the top ribbon so she could see the address. "Ethan's father."

"I wondered about that, seeing as how the only Jacob Gallagher I know is a mite young."

Brenna laughed and nodded. "Not for long, much to my dismay. Jacob Gallagher in Texas from a Victoria Ashworth also of Texas. Curious. Where did you find these?"

"Stuck between drawers in the bureau. I had to pull the drawer out to find them." She pointed to the torn edges. "That's how they ripped."

"Don't worry about that." Brenna sifted through the first few letters. "Whatever prompted you to look for them?"

Catie brushed her nose against Jacob's, encouraging a giggle. Jacob happily complied and twisted his fingers into her loose curls. "It was a dream, or I think I was dreaming. There was a woman in the dream. She looked at the drawers twice. She looked outside, too, but I don't know what I was supposed to see out there because it was too dark. She didn't go away until I left the bed."

Brenna gathered Catie and Jacob beneath one arm, though Catie stood almost as tall as Brenna, and guided them from the nursery. "Ethan couldn't sleep, either. He's in his study, so why don't we pose the mystery to him."

The firelight glowed against Ethan's back. His head was bent low over the desk, his hand and pen moved smoothly over paper. Catie wondered if he heard them enter, but his sudden smile indicated that he had. Ethan finished his thought and set the pen aside. "My three favorite people and a welcome distraction."

Catie grinned. "Isn't your brother and sister your favorites, too?"

"Aren't they, and you've beat them off of the favorite list." Ethan rubbed the top of her head and then lifted Jacob out of Brenna's arms. He held him up high causing his son to release a peal of laughter. When Jacob was tucked against his chest, Ethan kissed his wife's cheek. "It's barely five o'clock. Why is my little trio not asleep?"

Brenna nudged Catie closer to Ethan. "Show him what you've found."

Catie passed Ethan the bundled letters. "They were in a drawer in the bedroom. I didn't mean to move them, but . . ." Catie's eyes shifted focus to the mantel. The fire's light illuminated everything above the hearth. On the mantel sat a photograph to which Catie pointed. "Who is that?"

Ethan glanced at Brenna and then turned to see what had

drawn Catie's attention. "She was my mother." He removed the framed portrait and handed it to Catie. "That was the last picture taken of her, right here at this ranch."

Catie's hand shook, for staring up at her was the face of the woman in her dream. She gazed up at Ethan. "I found those letters and showed them to Brenna. I thought they might be important."

Ethan held the letters near the lamp. "Let's see what we have here." The pallor of his face whitened and his breathing hitched. "From my mother to my father. I've never seen these. Brenna, will you please—"

Brenna lifted Jacob from Ethan's arms before he finished asking. Ethan strode to the other side of his desk and sat down. With great care, he untied the ribbon and spread the letters out. "Not just from my mother, but also to her. Christmas 1862. My father was in the war, and my mother was home alone with us. Perhaps I remember my grandparents—her parents—were with us that year." Ethan seemed to have forgotten that anyone else was in the room as he continued to recall memories from a distant past. He held one of the letters but did not open it. "My father's parents passed on when I was barely a few years old. My other grandparents were barely known to us, and we met them for the first time that winter when they came to stay."

Ethan lowered the letter and leaned back in his chair. "We have been through everything my parents left behind. How did you find these?"

Catie told him about her dream, hesitant to reveal that the woman from the picture showed her where to find them.

Ethan shook his head. "Mabel had to have known these were there, though I don't know why she would have kept them hidden." He rose and explained to Catie. "Mabel was with us for many years, and she ran the inside of the house." He winked at Brenna. "She passed away last winter. The room you're sleeping in was hers, and it hasn't been used since her passing. You're sure the woman in the portrait was the one in your dream?"

Catie nodded without a glance back at the image of Ethan's mother. "I won't ever forget her face. It was a kind face, and she smiled, but cried a little, too. I don't reckon I believe in ghosts like she does," Catie glanced sideways at Brenna and smiled, "but I know what I saw."

"I believe you, Catie. Dreams are powerful, and sometimes they come to us for a reason." Ethan removed one of the letters from the envelope and passed it to Brenna to read.

My dearest Jacob,

Tomorrow is Christmas, and I do not know when you'll receive this letter. I've been told that correspondence from Texas and other parts of the South don't always make it through the lines. I wonder where you are this night as I think of you. The war has tried to beat us into submission, but we will prevail. Our children are strong and continue to live their lives the way we've taught them. Eliza wanted to pick out the tree again, but your sons decided it was their turn, which was just as well because the parlor isn't large enough for the trees she likes to choose.

My parents arrived yesterday bearing gifts for everyone. They have asked to stay for a few weeks to spend time with their grandchildren, and I cannot object. We've had our differences, yet despite those I am grateful they are here and that our children will know them. I pray this war ends soon, so you may return to us. Ethan and Gabriel are too young to understand why they can't join you, and were Eliza a little older, I imagine she'd take up the fight with them.

I know we promised that we'd always be together on this holiday, and you are with us in spirit.

Stay strong, my love, for we are waiting for you, and will be here until we can welcome you home again. I know there's an angel

watching over you—all of us—for our story is not over.
Merry Christmas, my love.

With all my heart,
Victoria

Catie stood beside Ethan, and she thought he might have cried, but when she glanced up at him, it was his smile she noticed first. Brenna had shed some tears, but she, too, smiled.

Ethan hugged Catie close. "Thank you for finding these. They are an unexpected gift, and I'm grateful you had the courage to listen to our ghost." Ethan placed a soft kiss on Catie's head and wrapped his arms around them all.

19

The day before Christmas Eve, Amanda awoke hours before the sunrise and occupied her mind and hands with minor tasks around the cottage until the early sun pushed away the darkness. She had remained late in town to help Joanna and Tilly, but she planned to return to the ranch after dawn to finish preparations. Sleep had eluded her throughout the evening, and she welcomed the chance to move about in what daylight the pending storm might offer. Snow had fallen during the night and the gray clouds above threatened to release more before the day ended.

Anxiety thrashed her awake more than once, though for what reasons she could not fathom. She passed those restless hours by reading, but the words on the page were a blur. The holiday would be a success thanks to the ingenuity and excitement of everyone involved. Why, then, did her thoughts churn over and over until uncertainty clouded her hope?

When a reasonable hour had approached, Amanda left the cottage, and nearly tripped over her own boots when she missed a step on the way to the church, the only building in town large enough to host the party. She had volunteered to help the reverend with the decorations and carried with her a basket filled with the finished stars for each of the children, a project she and

Isabelle had been working on for the past two weeks. Otis had bored a hole at the point of each one so she could run twine through to create a loop. Amanda righted herself and proceeded to the church. The town was unusually quiet that morning compared to the bustle of days before.

A quick burst of cold air swept into the church and with it, Ben Stuart. "Reverend, we need the bell sounded. Cord Beckert has gone missing."

Amanda rushed forward even as Ben left the church. She hurried along behind him, the fresh snow thwarting her efforts to keep up. She called out his name. Ben spun around and caught her when she would have fallen.

"I'm sorry. Thank you."

"You should stay inside, Amanda."

"I want to help." Men and women emerged from homes and businesses.

"What's happened, Ben?" shouted Loren.

"A boy has gone missing. Cord Beckert. Last his ma knew, Cord had gone up to the mining camp, but no one there has seen him. Most of the men from Hawk's Peak are out looking, and we need volunteers."

One by one, the men of the town raised their hands. Ben nodded and called out, "Get your horses. We'll split up into two groups."

The men dispersed, and the women with children held them fast or ushered them back inside. Amanda placed a hand on Ben's arm before he could get on his horse. "How long has he been gone?"

"Most of the night." Ben released his hand from the saddle and reins and held Amanda by the shoulders. "Please stay here. It's too dangerous out there right now with the storm moving in."

She gripped his arm. "I can help. I'm stronger than I look,

and at least I can be of some comfort to Cord's mother."

It took longer than Amanda had expected to convince Ben to take her to the Beckert's homestead. Mrs. Beckert—Sarah—ran out the moment she heard them ride up. She attempted to choke back tears when she saw it wasn't her son. Ben dismounted and then helped Amanda from the back of his horse. "This is Miss Warren, and she is going to stay with you while we search for your son. We have able men from town out looking for him. There are folks in town who will keep a look out in case he manages to reach Briarwood. The best thing you can do is stay in case he comes home."

Amanda wrapped the smaller woman in her arms and held her steady while she continued to cry. "We'll be all right."

Ben swung up onto the back of his gelding, a tall red-colored horse with as much eagerness and energy as his rider. The horse pranced beneath him as Ben turned a single circle, his eyes steady on Amanda.

Again she reassured him, "We'll be all right. Go."

With one last measured gaze, he headed north, the powerful animal kicking up snow in his wake.

Catie sat on the rug with Andrew and Jacob. They rolled a wooden ball back and forth between them, Brenna helping Jacob. The shouts and hurried footsteps, followed by all but two of the men riding away from the ranch, had Catie thinking ever since they left. It was a boy, only a few years younger than her, somewhere alone out there. He had a mother, so what was his reason for leaving? It could have been her out there.

"Brenna, will they find that boy?"

"What boy?" Andrew asked.

"A boy who is lost. His name is Cord. Amanda and Mr. Dawson told me about him. He lives a ways outside of town with his mother," she said by way of explaining.

Brenna helped Jacob roll the ball back to Andrew. "They won't stop looking until they do, Catie."

"Amanda said that Mr. Colton was going to bring Cord and his ma to the Christmas party. I hope nothing has happened to him." Images of what her own circumstances might have been this winter had the Gallaghers not found her filled her thoughts. She didn't want to think of someone like her out there alone.

Brenna looked over her shoulder when Isabelle came into the room. "Catie, they will find him safe. I'm certain of it."

Isabelle sat between Andrew and Catie, tucking her legs beneath the skirts of her dress. Andrew looked up at his sister. "Remember when those bad men took me, Ibby? Gabriel found me, and I wasn't too scared because I knew he would come." The young boy faced Catie. "They'll find him, Catie, you'll see."

Colton met Ethan and Ben at the ridge between the small-scale mining camp and the Beckert's homestead. Ben was inspecting the area through a looking glass. "See anything on your way up, Colton?"

"Nothing yet. I passed Gabriel on my way here; they're taking the north area."

"Do you think the boy could have traveled that far on his own?" Ethan asked.

"He had a mule with him," Colton explained. "He could have gotten farther than we realize, but if I had to guess, he's closer to the mining camp. There's a secondary trail—not used much— on the way to the camp. It would have been easy enough for him to veer off without realizing it. The other men from town are riding inward, and if the boy is up that way, then at least one of the groups will spot him."

Ben placed the looking glass in his saddlebag and glanced up at the sky. "Better sooner than later. Another night out in this weather, and he'll be frozen by morning."

"Let's make sure that doesn't happen," Ethan said. "Colton, I haven't been up this way in years. You take the lead."

The men rode northeast, following the camp road until they reached the point where the trail diverged. Colton held up his hand and dismounted.

Ethan glanced down at the snow. "Take a look."

Colton scooped away the top layer of snow and nodded. "Hoof prints." He remounted and they continued onward, up a slope and into the forest. The snowpack diminished in the heavy trees, allowing them to move at an easier pace. They lost the trail half a mile into the trees.

Ben pulled his horse up alongside Colton. "Maybe he backtracked and took another path through the forest."

Ethan shook his head and looked to Colton. "He's still in the forest."

Colton nodded. "I know these woods; there aren't any cabins nearby, but there is a cave some folks around here know about." He changed course and led the men east, deeper into the trees. Behind thick bushes and a fallen log stood the entrance. Ethan and Colton dismounted, handing their reins to Ben. Colton kept his rifle pointed to the ground, and remained alert.

"I met with a bear once outside this cave. Lucky for me, he was more interested in the berries than in me." Colton crouched and brushed aside a small area. "The mule's tracks. The cave is tall enough for a horse."

Ethan called out, "Cord Beckert! Are you there, son?"

No response.

With Ethan covering him, Colton headed first into the cave and swore. Huddled between the cave wall and his mule, Cord lay unconscious. "Ethan!"

Ethan rushed in behind him and coaxed the mule to stand.

Colton knelt beside the boy and checked for a heartbeat. Still breathing. The boy's eyes opened to narrow slits. His lips, a pale blue, moved slightly before his eyes closed again. Colton lifted the limp boy's body into his arms and carried him out of the cave. Ethan dropped the mule's reins and caught the canteen Ben tossed to him. He opened the boy's mouth and dripped water down his throat.

Ethan said, "We don't have time to make a fire. That storm is going to move in and trap us up here."

Colton nodded and carried the boy to Ben, who cradled Cord in his arms. Ethan took the blanket tied to his saddle and covered the boy. Colton did the same with his blanket and swung up on his horse. "We'll ride in front and behind," Ethan said and looked to Colton. "You take them to the homestead, and I'll head off Gabriel's group so that they know to stop looking."

Ethan rode ahead of them, and Colton knew that once he made it back to the forked road, he'd cover the distance in half the time it was going to take them. Colton took the lead, every few minutes searching the area around and behind Ben. He glanced back at the boy in Ben's arms more than once, until Ben assured him that Cord still breathed and his body was starting to warm up.

They reached the Beckert homestead three hours later. Colton's relief was immediate when he spotted the wagon and team in front of the modest house and Gabriel out front with Jackson. The short winter day guaranteed they only had enough daylight to get back into Briarwood, but with the wagon, they'd at least have a safe mode of travel for the boy and his mother.

Colton jumped down from his horse when they stopped. Gabriel reached Ben's horse first and lifted the boy into his arms.

"Did Ethan find you?" Colton asked.

Gabriel nodded. "He and Henry split up to let the other two groups know you found him." He carried the boy into the house and laid him out on a cot by the fire. Amanda rose and fetched an extra blanket to cover Cord.

"He's half-frozen." She knelt beside the narrow bed. "Gabriel, would you please hand me that kettle on the stove?" Ben saw that Amanda had been prepared for this moment. She poured some of the hot water into a serviceable bowl and dipped a clean rag in the water. She twisted the cloth to remove the excess water and smoothed it over Cord's forehead.

Ben knelt next to her and placed his hand on the blanket covering the boy's leg. "He'll have a tough time of it for a couple of days, but he'll be all right."

Gabriel poured another stream of water into the bowl before replacing the kettle on the stove. "We've seen a lot worse. Ben's right. The boy will make it." To Colton he said, "We'll leave within the hour."

Amanda paused in her ministrations. "You're moving him?"

Taking Amanda aside, Ben whispered, "They can't stay here. Cord needs the doctor and a warm place to recover. There are too many drafts in this house, and I'd wager not much in the cupboards. Don't worry, we'll get him to town safely."

Amanda wet a second cloth and trailed it over Cord's exposed neck and hands. "His mother worried herself in a faint. She's been asleep for half an hour, and I didn't want to wake her yet. Sarah blames herself for what happened. In her fit of tears, she confessed that they were out of what little money she'd managed to squander before her husband left, and the larder is near to empty."

"Does she know why Cord left?"

"Sarah believes he was going to the mining camp to look for work. She didn't know he'd left until she woke and found him gone."

"He's only twelve."

Amanda nodded. "You're sure he'll make it?"

Ben covered her hand with his. "He'll make it." A quick study of the small space indicated that there wouldn't be much to move. "Can you gather what you think they'll need to get by for a couple of days? We'll come back after Christmas for the rest of their things, but the new place should now have everything they'll require."

Amanda allowed Ben to help her stand. "After this, I don't believe you'll have any trouble convincing Sarah to accept her new home."

20

Catie worked alongside Amanda under her direction in the kitchen, rolling out dough, stirring sauces, and mixing the fruit fillings for pies. They depleted half of their store of canned fruits, and Kevin had assured them they there was plenty of meat in the springhouse when Elizabeth asked him to check on their supply. Catie had never seen so much food in one place, and she was in awe at the women's ability to create so many things from a few ingredients.

By the time the sun began to fade, they'd prepared half a dozen pies, three cakes—including the spice cake Loren was so fond of—more loaves of bread than Catie imagined anyone would ever need—and had added a dozen jars of canned vegetables to the bounty. All the while, Catie thought of the missing boy. She could be the one lost and alone in the snowy wilderness, uncertain of where to go or who to trust, if not for the Gallaghers. She sent up a silent prayer of thanks for herself and one of hope for Cord Beckert.

They hadn't heard anything from the rescue parties all day. Tommy Jr. and Kevin, two of the ranch hands, remained close to the house because there were horses and cattle to look after, but it seemed they, too, wished to help search for the boy.

An hour after sunset, the family had gathered around the

kitchen table, waiting anxiously for news of the men and the young boy. Dinner had been a simple affair where none of the adults ate much more than a few bites, too restless for news to fully enjoy the meal. Andrew left the table shortly after the meal to play with his puppy. The wind and snow had stopped, making it easier to hear someone's approach. It wasn't long before they heard the sound of riders, and Catie was the first out of her chair. She rushed outside, forgetting a coat in the process.

Ramsey stood next to his horse, and upon seeing her, slipped out of his coat and wrapped it over her shoulders. "It's too cold out here. Come on back inside"

She ignored him. "Did you find him?"

"Colton, Ethan, and Ben found him. He's back home with his mother now." Ramsey guided her into the house, Ethan and Gabriel close on their heels.

"Will he be all right?"

Ramsey ruffled Catie's long brown hair. "He's going to be better than all right."

After the energy mellowed, and everyone had gathered together in the living room, they told the family who had found Cord Beckert and how. They assured them the boy would recover, and he and his mother were now safely in town and in a new home, generously rented by an unknown benefactor. Catie had more questions—many of them—but she'd wait. She stared up at the empty tree waiting to be decorated and wondered if Cord had one of his own.

"Come quick, Catie! It's time!"

"Time for what? Breakfast?" Andrew had burst in and out of the bedroom. "Andrew?" Curious, Catie laid down her book and followed him down the stairs and into the spacious living room where the family tree stood tall near a window. There stood the family, each member peering into boxes or sipping on hot beverages. Elizabeth and Amanda laughed when Amanda held up a wooden bowl filled with strings of berries and popped corn. Andrew munched on a cookie while holding up an ornament for Isabelle to see.

Brenna walked to Catie and draped an arm over her shoulders. "We wanted the whole family to be here before we began."

Catie peered up at Brenna and felt her eyes moisten. Brenna brushed a kiss over her cheek, squeezed her shoulders, and said, "Come on. I think Andrew could use your help choosing where to place the ornaments."

Together they walked to the tree. Elizabeth handed her a cookie and cup of cocoa before she held up her hands to fend off a kernel of popped corn Ramsey tossed over the group. Ramsey grinned and then laughed when Eliza pinched his side. Strings of dried berries intertwined with glass balls and other small ornaments from different parts of the country. Brenna's family in Scotland sent her a wooden crate of the decorations she and her parents had used when she was younger. Amanda served hot cider, and Isabelle played songs on the piano as the family decorated the tree.

A tiny candle perched on the edges of the sturdier branches, but they didn't light them yet. Catie stepped back when Gabriel secured the final candle near the top. "It's the most beautiful tree I've ever seen."

"It's not finished yet," Ethan said. Brenna unwrapped a delicate figure wearing a sparkling white and gold dress, and on its back, wings.

"This belonged to my mother, and came all the way from Scotland." Brenna handed the angel to Catie. "Will you do the honor of placing her on the top?"

Astonished, Catie accepted the angelic figure. "She's perfect."

Ethan knelt beside Catie and said, "Are you ready?"

She nodded and laughed when Ethan hoisted her onto his shoulder. Gabriel stood on the other side of her, and together he and Ethan lifted her in their strong arms until she could reach the top of the tree. Catie secured the angel, and when they lowered her back down, Ramsey and Eliza lit the first candles, setting the angel aglow.

Isabelle sat back down at the piano, and with nimble fingers played "Angels We Have Heard on High," while the family joined in the song. They moved onto "One Horse Open Sleigh" with boisterous voices and a bit of laughter when Andrew sang the chorus with enthusiastic gusto.

The following day on Christmas Eve, Catie was the second person in the household who awakened. The entire family, including Ramsey and Eliza, had slept beneath one roof, filling the house to capacity. Andrew was already in the living room on the rug by the tree. His puppy lay curled up next to him, sleeping. Catie added two small logs to the fire and joined Andrew. "I've never seen a tree so big, have you?"

Andrew peered upward. "I think so. In New Orleans, we had a big tree at Christmas, but we didn't get to decorate it."

"Who did?"

"Mother called them the servants, but Ibby said it's not nice to call people that."

Catie stroked the thick hair on the puppy. "I've never had a Christmas tree before."

Andrew didn't mock her as other young boys might. Instead, he leaned into her and laid his head on her shoulder. "It's all right, Catie. This is going to be the best Christmas ever, you'll see."

The rest of the household trickled downstairs over the next

two hours. Some went outside to handle chores around the ranch, others spent the morning in the kitchen preparing breakfast and gathering all of the food they'd baked into one place for easier loading into the wagons. The tree decorating in town was planned for noon, and the church would be prepared for everyone to enjoy a hot meal and the company of neighbors.

Most importantly, Catie wanted to meet new friends. She'd never had one before—not her own age. Isabelle warned her that most of the students in town would be younger, but Catie didn't mind. For the first time in her in life, she knew what it meant to have a home and a family who would never leave her.

Joanna and Tilly had successfully spread the word about each person or family adding a special memory to the tree. Lockets and dolls, hand-carved toys, and small family trinkets, were scattered over the lower half of the tree. The fierce storm they had expected to envelope the valley through Christmas continued south, leaving the town just enough time to decorate what they could of the tree.

Ribbon had been interwoven with the branches, and a light dusting still lingered to give them a snow-kissed tree. The Gallagher family and ranch hands climbed out of wagons and off their horses, greeting the townspeople and then transporting their offerings to the church. Two long wooden tables filled the center of the room where the church benches normally sat. Half of the tables had already been filled with sweets and savories provided by other families.

Catie proudly placed the pies she had helped bake onto the table, and then Brenna encouraged her to run along and join the other children by the tree.

"You're coming, too."

"We'll be along soon." Brenna handed Catie the three items the family had agreed upon. A photograph of Jacob and Victoria Gallagher when Hawk's Peak was first built. A broach Brenna's father gave to her mother at Brenna's first Christmas. And a silver snowflake Isabelle and Andrew made to represent a new beginning and the start of new traditions. "Will you hang these on the tree for us?"

Catie held the items with reverence and nodded. She hurried over the snow as quickly as her boots—new boots Brenna had surprised her with that morning—to the small crowd around the tree. It was cold work, but Tilly served cider, coffee, and hot chocolate to those standing outside. Catie turned her back to the throng and noise and one by one placed each item on the tree. She then searched her pocket for her mother's silver locket and hung it from a branch. Her fingers held onto the necklace for a minute.

"It's beautiful."

Catie turned to find Amanda beside her. "It was my ma's." Catie looked at Amanda's hands. "Did you bring something?"

"I did. From my mother." Amanda wrapped her arm over Catie's shoulders. "I'd like you to meet someone." Without further explanation and with a covered basket over her other arm, Amanda walked Catie down the road to the single house where the Beckerts now lived. "Go ahead and knock."

Uncertain who she'd find on the other side, she cast the teacher a curious look and knocked. After a few seconds, a woman answered. Amanda smiled and introduced them. "Mrs. Beckert, this is Catie Carr. She'll be in class with Cord after the holidays."

Sarah Beckert took Catie's hand in her own and brushed aside a few strands of mousey brown hair. "It's wonderful to meet you, Catie, and to see you again, Miss Warren. I wasn't in a position to thank you properly for what you did for me and my boy."

Amanda only smiled again and asked, "Is Cord well enough to receive visitors?"

Sarah nodded and stepped aside. "Of course. Please come

inside." She led them into a small bedroom off the kitchen. It was sparse but clean. The woodstove in the kitchen warmed the entire home. Cord sat up in bed, a bowl of soup on the table beside him. "We were just having our lunch."

Amanda held out the basket. "I thought since Cord couldn't come to the town's party, we'd bring a little of it to him."

Sarah humbly accepted the basket, her face brighter and cleaner than Amanda suspected it had been in a long time. "Thank you. Cord was disappointed that he couldn't go today."

"Ma says I ain't well enough yet," Cord offered, though his eyes had centered on Catie. "Hi. Who are you?"

Amanda ushered Sarah back into the kitchen, allowing Catie to take care of her own introduction. "Catherine Rose, but most folks call me Catie." She looked around the tidy room and thought how lucky he was. "You made the whole town worry about you."

Cord stared down at this hands. "I know. Ma says I got to say sorry to everyone."

"They weren't mad at you." Catie sat down in the chair next to the bed. "Why did you run away?"

Cord's heavy sigh carried a weight of guilt. "I reckoned I could get work at the mining camp. Ma's been awful worried since Pa left."

"Where'd he go?"

Cord shrugged. "Don't know. He said he was going to find work, took the wagon and horse, and never came back."

Catie could sympathize. "My pa left, too, but then the Gallaghers found me. I don't know what I would've done if they hadn't." She cocked her head and studied him. "How old are you?"

"Twelve. How old are you?"

"Thirteen." Catie could now say her age and know it was true.

Cord's sympathetic gaze said he understood. "I forget my

birthday, too. Are you going to be in class when they get a new teacher?"

Catie nodded. "I have to learn a lot if I want to run a ranch someday."

Cord's eyes widened. "I ain't never heard of no girl running a ranch."

"Then you haven't met Eliza. She's the best rider in all of Montana, and she's a girl."

"Well, I reckon if a girl can ride good then she can maybe be the boss of a ranch. Can she shoot?"

Catie grinned. "Sure can. I know how to hunt, too."

Admiration and wonder filled Cord's expression. "My pa taught me all about huntin', but I ain't too good with riding."

"When you're better, you can come riding with me."

"Do you mean it?"

"I sure do." Catie pulled a cookie from her pocket. "I was saving this for later, but you should have it. It's one of Miss Amanda's oatmeal cookies. There isn't anything better."

Cord smiled and bit into the cookie. His smile widened. "I reckon there ain't nothing else better than that." He peered around Catie into the kitchen and then asked, "Will you tell me about the tree in town? Is it big?"

"Well, I'm no expert on trees, but I think it's the biggest and prettiest tree you ever saw." Catie told him all about the memories people had hung from the branches and the ribbons covering the tree. "Maybe someone can carry you to the tree, so you can hang your own memory on it."

Cord's smile faded. "I ain't got nothing."

Catie quieted and looked around the room. Save for a few articles of worn clothing hanging from hooks on the wall, the room was bare. "I know! Amanda?" Catie walked into the kitchen. "Can—may I go outside for a few minutes?"

Amanda studied Catie. "Of course you may."

Catie disappeared out the front door and returned five minutes later. She rushed past the kitchen and into the bedroom, taking a minute to calm her racing heart. "Hold out your hand, Cord." She pressed her ma's silver locket into Cord's open palm.

"What is it?"

Catie borrowed Isabelle's phrase and said, "A new beginning. Open it."

Cord released the locket's latch and opened it, but it was blank.

"When you and your ma get your pictures taken, you can put them inside the locket." What had Ramsey said about her future? "It's a blank canvas."

Cord didn't seem to entirely understand what she meant, but he gripped the locket in his hand and held it over his heart. "Thanks, Catie."

21

The sun had descended by the time they'd left the Beckert's home, but it had been time well spent. When Ethan came around looking for Catie, Amanda had assured him that all was well. He heard the children speaking inside, smiled, and returned to the church. Catie and Amanda walked side-by-side down the darkened road. The lamp Sarah had given them swung in Catie's grasp.

"Are you going to put your memory on the tree, Amanda?"

"I will."

"Can I see it?"

Amanda hesitated only briefly before removing a gold angel from her pocket. Attached to the wings was a long chain.

Catie touched the smooth surface of the angel's gown. "It's so pretty."

Amanda caressed the golden angel. "My father gave this to my mother many years ago."

Catie peered up at her. "It will look lovely on the tree."

Amanda placed the agent in Catie's hand. "Why don't you hang it for me?"

Awed, Catie accepted the small angel and hung it from the highest branch she could reach.

"It's perfect, thank you. Now go ahead to the party. I'll be along shortly."

With lantern in hand, Catie skipped over the snow, almost slipped, and then righted herself with a giggle and headed into the party.

Alone now, Amanda wasn't quite ready to go inside, needing a few minutes of solitude to reflect on what had happened at the Beckert's house. Many people waited their entire lives to witness a miracle, not realizing that they took place every day. The kindness toward strangers was a miracle in itself. One child was given a home and family, another was not forgotten. Those who had little, now stood with the rest of the town to rejoice in an abundance of generosity.

"Are you joining them?"

Amanda continued to gaze up at the evening stars. A soft smile touched her lips, red now from the cold. "Soon, but it's too peaceful out here to leave."

"I know what you mean."

She looked t Ben. "Why aren't you inside?"

He shrugged. "I was. Too many people."

Amanda laughed and listened to the carols sung by Reverend Philips small, but dedicated, choir. She didn't realize a tear had fallen from her eye until Ben brushed it away.

"What's wrong, Amanda?"

"Have you ever wanted something so much—more than you realized was even possible—but you didn't know how to get it?"

Ben contemplated her for a few minutes. "What is it you want more than anything?"

"Before I arrived in Briarwood, I . . ."

Ben held her by the shoulders, and then his hands moved down her arms until his fingers twined with hers. "You what?"

She exhaled a shuddering breath and stared into his eyes. "I ran from my own life in search of a new one. I found it here, but I worry every day that something from my past will destroy the life I have now."

"That's where you're wrong." Ben brushed away another single tear as it fell to her cheek. "We can do more than we believe ourselves capable of—I'm proof of that. Heck, if you don't believe it, look at Catie. If ever there was a person to inspire us all, it's that young girl. Don't run anymore, Amanda."

Amanda pulled back just enough to give herself a little clarity, but before her mind could clear away the emotional fog, Ben lowered his lips to hers, a faint meeting of hearts that lasted only a second but seared itself on her soul. When neither of them said anything, he stepped away from her and started toward the church. Amanda's own heartbeat felt foreign, as though it stopped keeping time the moment Ben walked away. Amanda released her tears and shed them silently as the stars twinkled in the dark winter sky. Her future was no longer clear but filled with uncertainty and excitement.

The warmth inside of her continued to burn strong, and everything became clear.

"Amanda." Ben said her name from a few feet away. Catie Carr and Cord Beckert weren't the only ones in need of a miracle that Christmas.

Ben stared at her in a way that made her wonder if time had stood still. He held out an arm, which she accepted. Together, they joined the Christmas celebration. The reverend had his nativity, complete with a real lamb. Andrew laughed as he tried to help Forest keep his dog from barking at the poor animal. Catie caught her eye and waved, and then returned to a conversation with a younger girl whose blond curls bounced beneath an assortment of colorful ribbons.

The choir consisted of only six members of the town, but what they lacked in numbers they made up for with enthusiasm. They segued from one carol to the next in a smooth transition, with the occasional child accompanying them. Gabriel's arm was wrapped around Isabelle's waist. She glowed as bright as the candles. Ramsey and Eliza filled two plates with food and carried them to an elderly couple sitting on one of the benches near the woodstove.

Elizabeth stood in the choir, her lyrical voice somewhat gravelly but as beautiful as the words from the song. Brenna leaned against Ethan, his arm around her shoulder and the other holding young Jacob. Colton and the other ranch hands mingled with the townspeople.

Two long tables lined the wall and were covered with the offerings not only from Hawk's Peak, but it would seem that every able person in town brought something. A small tree stood in the corner of one table, and on the branches, the stars Amanda and Isabelle had made for the children. When the townfolks had their fill of food and song, Otis invited them outside where three horse-drawn sleighs waited in front of the church. One by one, families, friends, and children gathered for their turn. Andrew pulled Catie to the nearest sleigh where they joined three other children. Catie stood on the step of the sleigh and grinned back at her family.

22

On Christmas morning, Catie sat cross-legged on the rug, as close to the tree as she could get in the great room, and found it difficult to contain her emotions. Gifts had appeared beneath the tree at some point during the night, and she admired the ribbons and colorful wrappings that adorned each one. Catie smiled wide as she reflected on how blessed she was to have already received the most perfect and unexpected Christmas gift.

The town's Christmas party was wonderful, and better than Catie had imagined, but the time alone with the family when they had returned home had meant more to her than any party or gift.

Alone with the tree and her own thoughts, Catie didn't hear the padding of feet behind her until Andrew was upon her. He sat down next to her and stared up at the tree. "Aunt Brenna and Uncle Ethan said you're going to live with them, so we get to play together still, right? You're not going away?"

Catie draped her arm around Andrew. "I'm not going away. I always wanted a little brother." They remained together, enjoying the quiet and warmth of each other's company. It wasn't long before the household stirred, and soon everyone was gathered in the great room. The scent of Amanda's sweet rolls wafted in when she joined them. Catie had been told that everyone, including the ranch hands, would come together for breakfast. No one moved to open presents. Instead, Ethan produced the bundled letters.

He sifted through them until he found the one he wanted. To the family he explained, "We'll get to the presents shortly, but Catie has discovered something in this house that may very well be the best Christmas present we've had in years." He shifted his focus to Eliza and Gabriel. "Letters between Mother and Father when Father was away in the war. I've read one of them, and I'd like to read it now to all of you."

Catie listened to the familiar words and wished she could read words written by her ma. Ethan finished the letter and then passed the others around for the family to read. Some laughed, others cried, but it was the best Christmas present they could have received.

Eliza folded the last letter and slipped it into the envelope. "How did you find these, Catie?"

Catie shrugged. "The ghost."

Silence ensued, and all eyes shifted to Catie.

Eliza smirked. "I heard about our friendly ghost. Has anyone heard anything in the last couple of days?"

Everyone looked around, but no one could recall that they had.

Brenna said, "I haven't heard anything since . . ." Brenna looked at Catie, "since the letters were found."

Elizabeth held Jacob on her lap and smoothed down his dark hair. "My grandmother used to tell me stories of ghosts. She came from England and worked in a great castle reputed to be haunted. No one claimed to have seen the ghosts until one autumn night she looked out a tower window and saw a pale figure sweep across the pond. It was a young boy, and she saw him each night for a week. Later, she discovered a painting in the lord and lady's bedroom of the same young boy who had drowned in that very pond ten years earlier. The lady told my grandmother that her son visited every year during the week of his birthday, but no one else had ever seen him before my grandmother."

In awe, Catie asked, "Why did he come back?"

"Oh, we can't know that." Elizabeth winked at Brenna. "Sometimes a spirit isn't ready to let go, or perhaps they have something to say, a gift to give." She nodded toward the bundle of letters Ethan held once more. "Why did you find the letters, Catie, and no one else?"

Catie looked around the room at the warm smiles and glistening eyes of her family. Why had Victoria Gallagher come to her?

Eliza said, "I'm grateful our mother showed herself to Catie. These letters brought them back to us during a time when we have so much to celebrate."

"I think it's more than that." Gabriel leaned back into the settee and wrapped his arm around Isabelle. "I believe it was our mother's way of welcoming Catie into the family."

Catie leaped from her chair and forced a loud whoosh out of Gabriel when she landed next to him and wrapped her arms around his waist.

"Now that's what I call a welcome to the family," Ethan said.

A soft smile touched Catie's lips, and her heart skipped a beat. She returned to Brenna's side and leaned into her embrace. "If ghosts are real, can angels be real, too?"

"What do you think?"

Catie glanced at Ethan who held Andrew on his lap. "I think an angel helped Ethan find me that day."

Everyone smiled, and Amanda said, "Then what they say is true, Christmas angels do exist."

Ethan passed the bundle of letters to Catie. "I believe these are meant for you as much for us. Why don't you get to know your grandparents?"

Later that evening when she was tucked away in her bedroom, she pulled a chair beside the frosted window. With the curtains open and a warm fire glowing behind her, Catie opened another of Victoria's letters.

Thank you for reading *An Angel Called Gallagher*.
Scroll through for a glimpse at the next Gallagher novel and Elizabeth Hunter's Spiced Apple & Cranberry Cake.

Visit mkmcclintock.com/extras for more on the Gallagher family, Hawk's Peak, and Briarwood.

If you enjoyed this story, please consider sharing your thoughts with fellow readers by leaving an online review.

Don't miss out on future books!
www.mkmcclintock.com/subscribe

Don't miss *Journey to Hawk's Peak*, book five of the Montana Gallagher series.

JOURNEY TO HAWK'S PEAK

Book Five of the Montana Gallagher Series

One woman's desperation to escape will become the greatest journey of her life.

Amanda Warren arrives in Briarwood, Montana, with one satchel and a dream. After death destroyed her happiness, she flees, unwilling to believe it is the end, yet her weary spirit thinks only of survival.

Then she meets the Gallaghers.

They take a chance and give her a home and a family, but is she strong enough to make a new start?

Ben Stuart has seen more of life than he wants to remember, but with the Gallaghers he has found a place where he can forget times gone by and live the life he always wanted. When Amanda arrives at Hawk's Peak, Ben sees a woman hiding from secrets and running from her past. How will he convince her that the journey is over?

Join us on a journey to Hawk's Peak for a romantic adventure you'll never forget.

"... one of the most gripping and thrilling western novels that anyone will ever read. This is probably the best novel that I have yet read as a reviewer. This novel is a serious page-turner, and for fans of western fiction, it is a must-read."
—*Readers' Favorite*

CHARACTER GUIDE

View the full Gallagher family tree and Briarwood Character Guide on the author's website.

Ethan Gallagher	*m.* Brenna Cameron in *Gallagher's Pride*
Gabriel Gallagher	*m.* Isabelle Rousseau in *Gallagher's Hope*
Eliza Gallagher	*m.* Ramsey Hunter in *Gallagher's Choice*
Ramsey Hunter	Twin brother to Brenna Gallagher
Andrew Rousseau	Younger brother to Isabelle Gallagher
Jacob Gallagher	First son born to Ethan and Brenna
Mabel	Original Housekeeper at Hawk's Peak
Elizabeth Hunter	*m.* Nathan Hunter
	Grandmother to Brenna and Ramsey
Nathan Hunter	Grandfather to Brenna and Ramsey
Amanda Warren	Housekeeper, friend, and cook at Hawk's
Peak	
Ben Stuart	Ranch foreman at Hawk's Peak
Colton Dawson	Ranch hand at Hawk's Peak
Jackson & Jake	Ranch hands at Hawk's Peak
Catherine Rose Carr	Young girl in *An Angel Called Gallagher*
Joseph Carr	Catie's father
Cyrus Carr	Catie's Uncle
Reverend Phillips	Town reverend
Orin Lloyd	Telegraph operator
Forest Lloyd	Orin's son
Otis Lincoln	Blacksmith and livery owner
Tilly	Café owner
Loren Baker	General Store Owner
Joanna Baker	Loren's wife
Cord Beckert	Young boy in *An Angel Called Gallagher*
Sarah Beckert	Cord's mother

Elizabeth Hunter's
Spiced Apple & Cranberry Cake

Cake:
3 cups flour
1 cup sugar
1 ½ tsp baking soda
½ tsp salt
1 tsp cinnamon
½ tsp allspice
¼ tsp nutmeg
1 cup buttermilk
½ cup (1 stick) unsalted butter, melted
2 large egg whites
2 cups chopped apples
½ cup dried cranberries
½ cup chopped pecans

Glaze (optional):
¼ cup unsalted butter, melted
2 cups powdered sugar
2-5 Tbs. non-fat milk (depending upon the consistency you prefer)
2 tsp pure vanilla extract

Directions:
1. In a large bowl, combine flour, sugar, baking soda, salt, cinnamon, allspice, and nutmeg.
2. Stir in buttermilk, butter, and egg just until combined.

3. Fold in apples, cranberries, and pecans just until combined; pour into sprayed* bundt pan (or 13 x 9 pan).
4. Bake at 325 degrees F for 45-55 minutes or until done.**
5. To make the glaze, combine the melted butter, powdered sugar, and 2 Tbs. of milk. Blend in the vanilla extract. Add additional milk based on the consistency you prefer.

*In this recipe, sprayed refers to the use of Baker's Joy Baking Spray with Flour. If you don't mind the extra calories, you can butter and flour the pan. Once upon a time, they would have used lard (our shortening) but I would not recommend it.

**Oven temps may vary, so check the cake after 45 minutes as it's easy to overbake. If you can insert a knife and have it come out completely clean, then you've overbaked the cake. The cake will continue to bake for a few minutes once removed from the oven. When inserting a knife it should come out mostly clean.

ABOUT THE AUTHOR

Award-winning author MK McClintock writes historical romantic fiction about chivalrous men and strong women who appreciate chivalry. Her stories of adventure, romance, and mystery sweep across the American West to the Victorian British Isles, with places and times between and beyond. With her heart deeply rooted in the past, she enjoys a quiet life in the northern Rocky Mountains.

MK invites you to join her on her writing journey at www.mkmcclintock.com, where you can read the blog, explore reader extras, and sign up to receive new release updates.

Discussion questions for MK's novels are available at her website.

Printed in Great Britain
by Amazon

14472795R00123